2x 9/15 LT 5/15

WITHDR

D0340681

# SHOPLIFTER

MICHAEL CHO

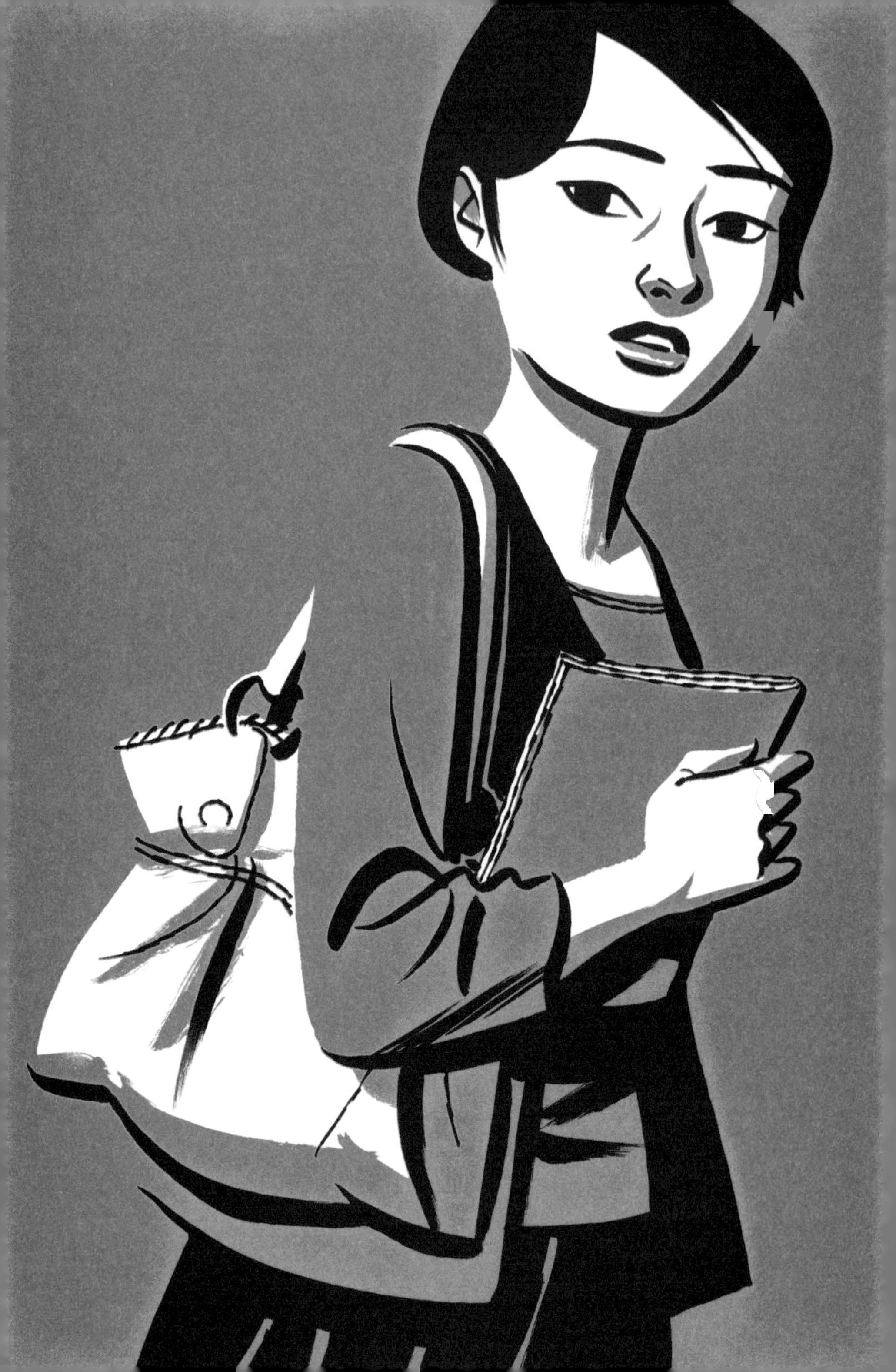

# SHOPLIFTER

MICHAEL CHO

PANTHEON BOOKS
NEW YORK

This is a work of fiction. Names, characters, places, and incidents either are the product of the author's imagination or are used fictitiously. Any resemblance to actual persons, living or dead, events, or locales is entirely coincidental.

Copyright © 2014 by Michael Cho

Book Design by Claudia Dávila and Michael Cho

All rights reserved. Published in the United States by Pantheon Books, a division of Random House LLC, New York, and in Canada by Random House of Canada Limited, Toronto, Penguin Random House companies.

Pantheon Books and colophon are registered trademarks of Random House LLC.

Library of Congress Cataloging-in-Publication Data
Cho, Michael
Shoplifter / Michael Cho.
pages   cm
HC ISBN 978-0-307-91173-5. EBK ISBN 978-0-307-91174-2.
1. Self-realization in women—Comic books, strips, etc. 2. Shoplifting—Comic books, strips, etc. 3. Graphic novels. I. Title.
PN6733.C58S56 2014     741.5'971—dc23     2014003490

www.pantheonbooks.com

Printed in the United States of America
First Edition
9 8 7 6 5 4 3 2 1

*For Yolanda*

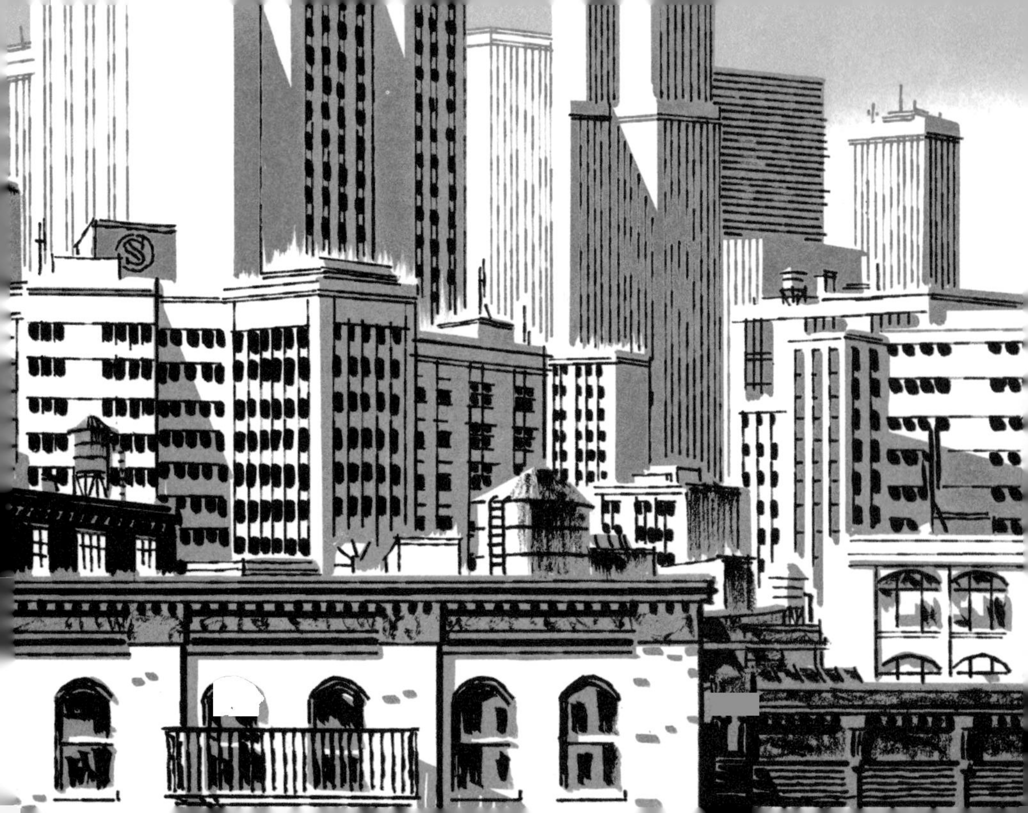

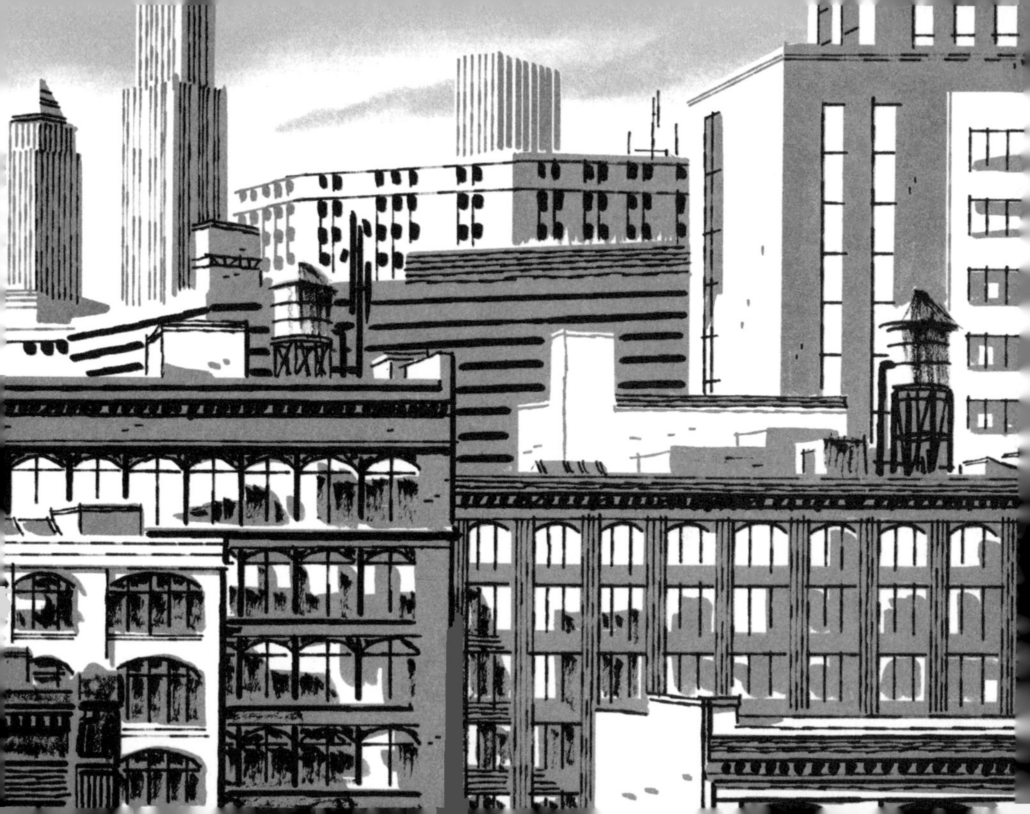

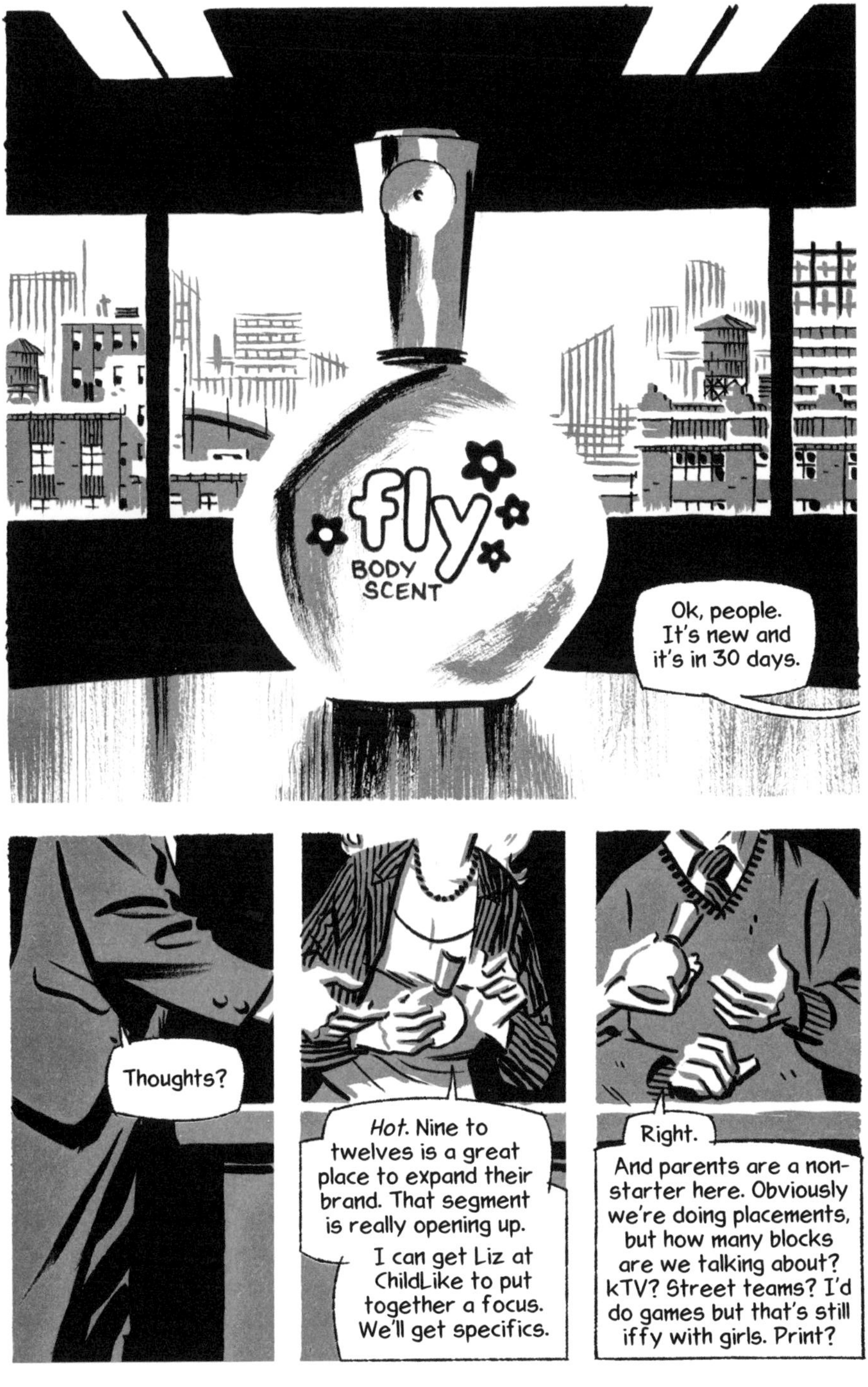
fly
BODY SCENT
Ok, people. It's new and it's in 30 days.
Thoughts?
*Hot*. Nine to twelves is a great place to expand their brand. That segment is really opening up.
I can get Liz at ChildLike to put together a focus. We'll get specifics.
Right.
And parents are a non-starter here. Obviously we're doing placements, but how many blocks are we talking about? kTV? Street teams? I'd do games but that's still iffy with girls. Print?

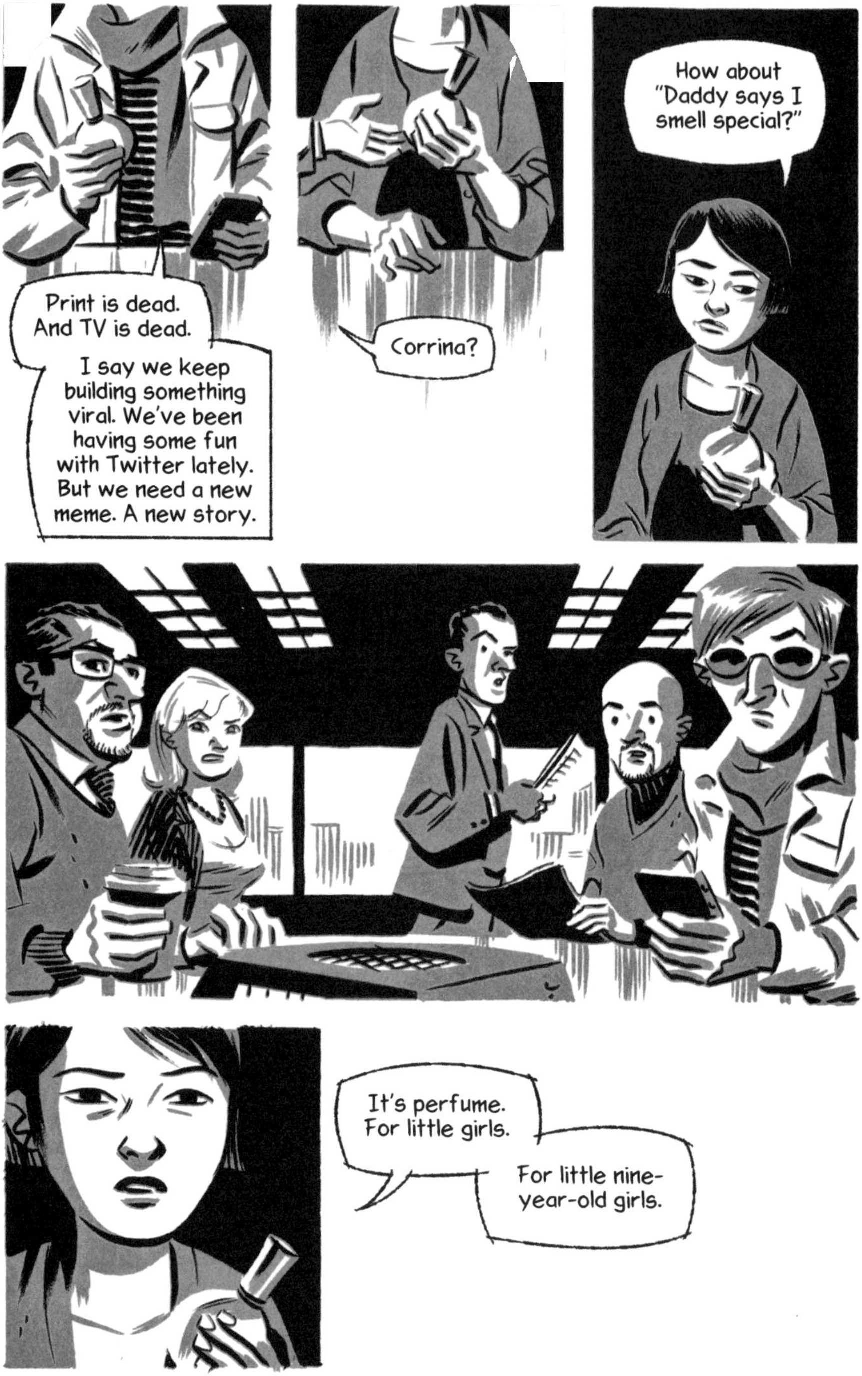
Print is dead. And TV is dead.
I say we keep building something viral. We've been having some fun with Twitter lately. But we need a new meme. A new story.
Corrina?
How about "Daddy says I smell special?"
It's perfume. For little girls.
For little nine-year-old girls.

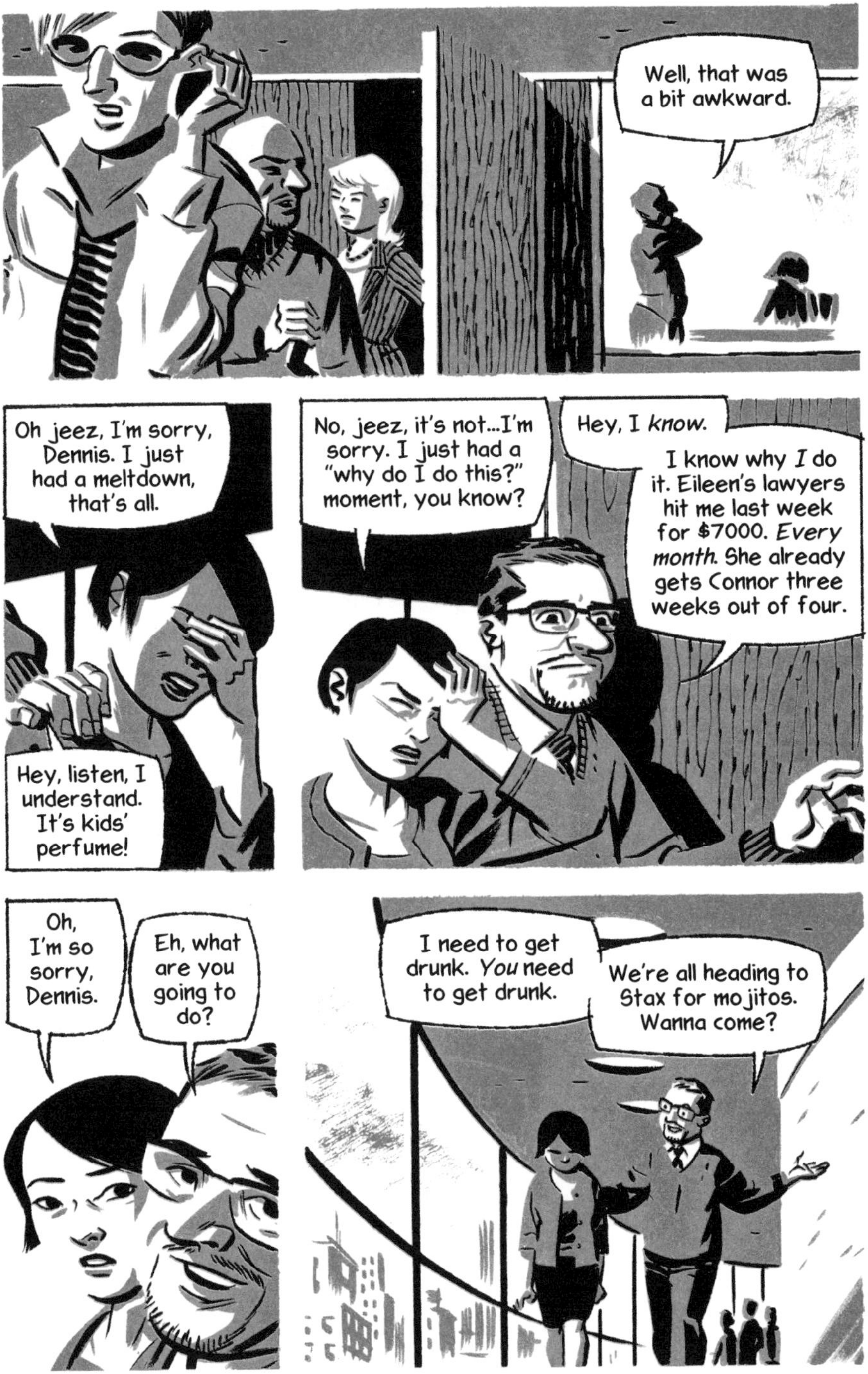
Well, that was a bit awkward.
Oh jeez, I'm sorry, Dennis. I just had a meltdown, that's all.
Hey, listen, I understand. It's kids' perfume!
No, jeez, it's not...I'm sorry. I just had a "why do I do this?" moment, you know?
Hey, I *know*.
I know why *I* do it. Eileen's lawyers hit me last week for $7000. *Every month*. She already gets Connor three weeks out of four.
Oh, I'm so sorry, Dennis.
Eh, what are you going to do?
I need to get drunk. *You* need to get drunk.
We're all heading to Stax for mojitos. Wanna come?

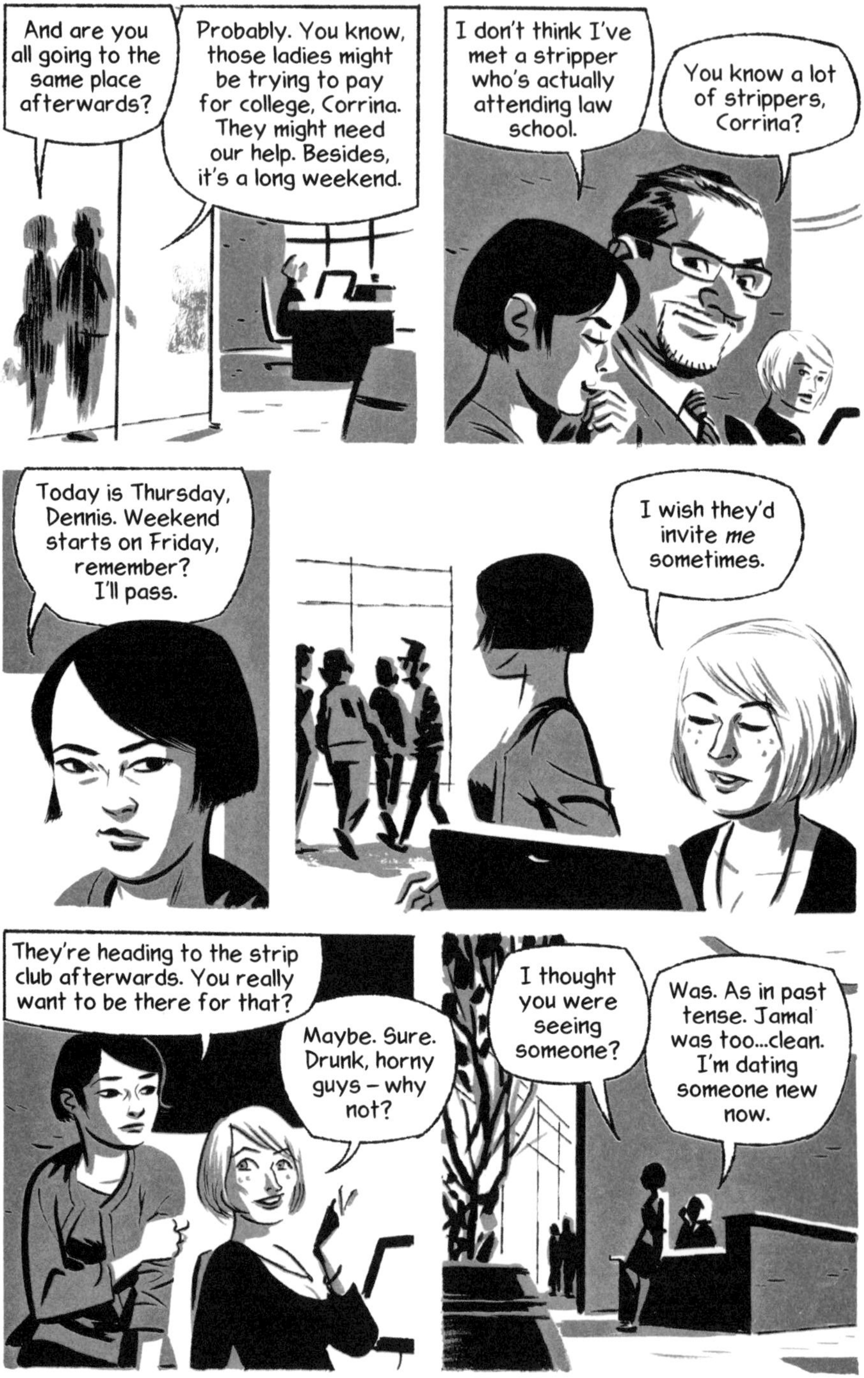
And are you all going to the same place afterwards?
Probably. You know, those ladies might be trying to pay for college, Corrina. They might need our help. Besides, it's a long weekend.
I don't think I've met a stripper who's actually attending law school.
You know a lot of strippers, Corrina?
Today is Thursday, Dennis. Weekend starts on Friday, remember? I'll pass.
I wish they'd invite *me* sometimes.
They're heading to the strip club afterwards. You really want to be there for that?
Maybe. Sure. Drunk, horny guys – why not?
I thought you were seeing someone?
Was. As in past tense. Jamal was too...clean. I'm dating someone new now.

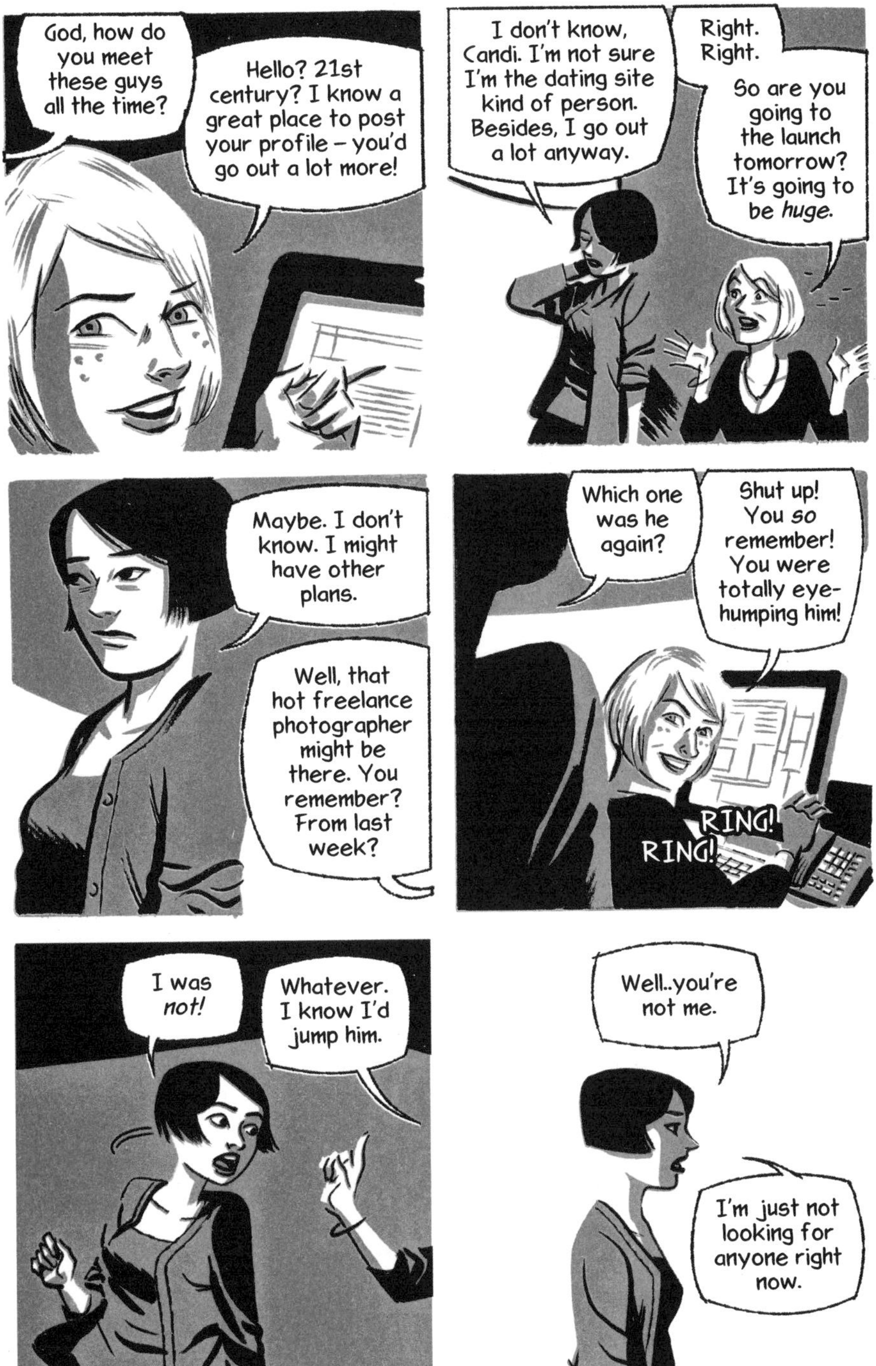
God, how do you meet these guys all the time?
Hello? 21st century? I know a great place to post your profile – you'd go out a lot more!
I don't know, Candi. I'm not sure I'm the dating site kind of person. Besides, I go out a lot anyway.
Right. Right.
So are you going to the launch tomorrow? It's going to be *huge*.
Maybe. I don't know. I might have other plans.
Well, that hot freelance photographer might be there. You remember? From last week?
Which one was he again?
Shut up! You so remember! You were totally eye-humping him!
RING!
RING!
I was *not!*
Whatever. I know I'd jump him.
Well..you're not me.
I'm just not looking for anyone right now.

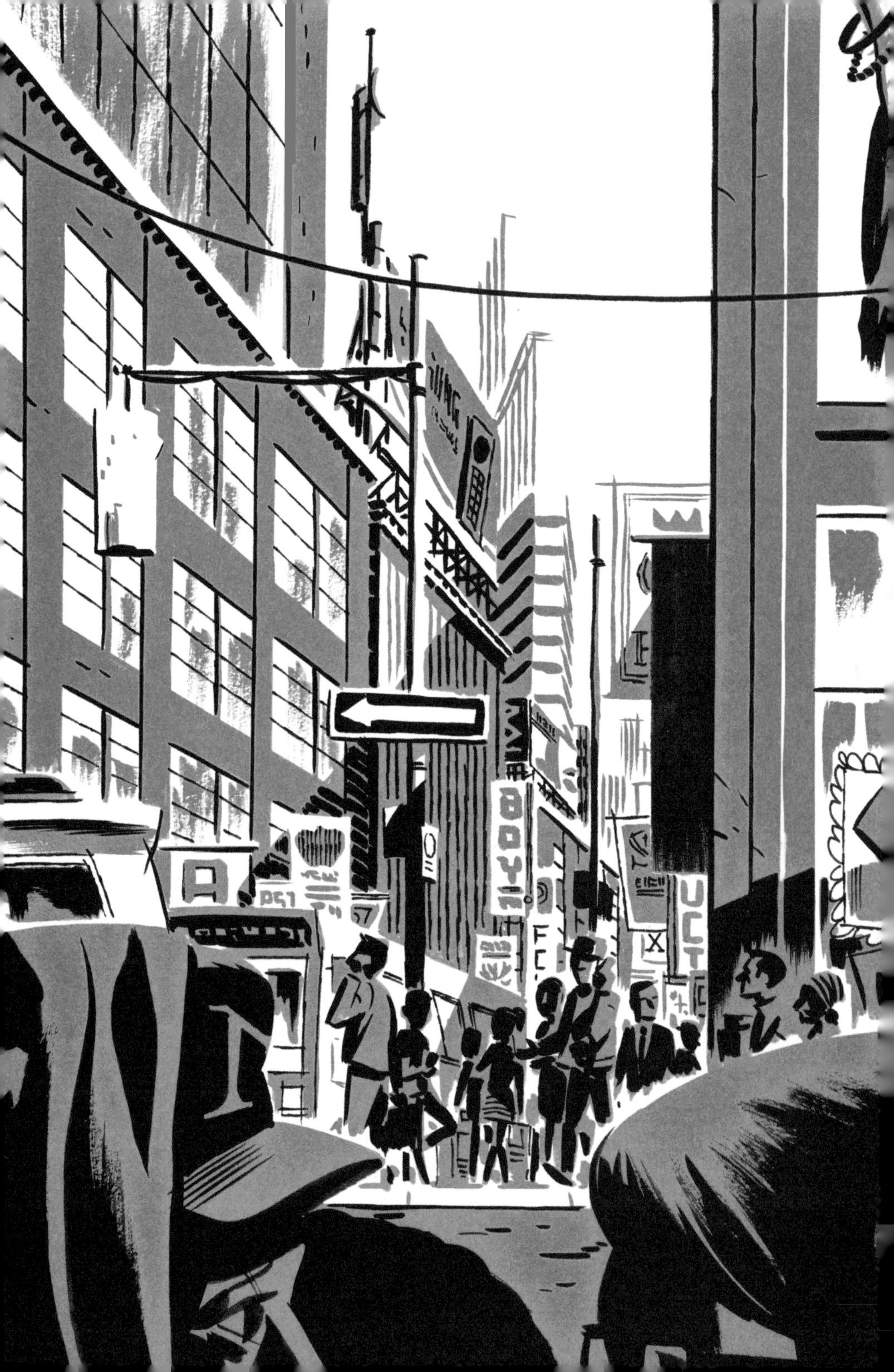

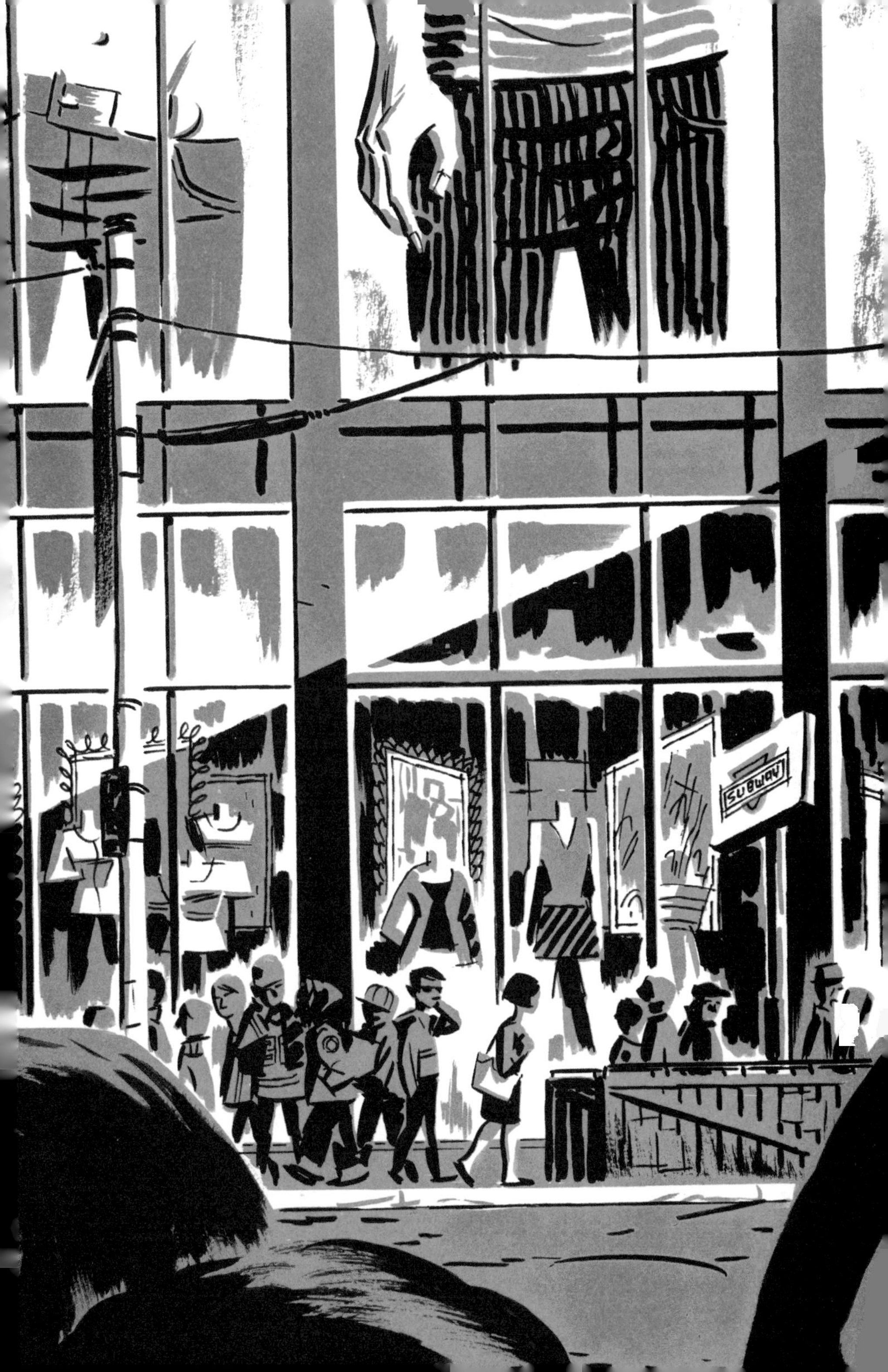
SUBWAY

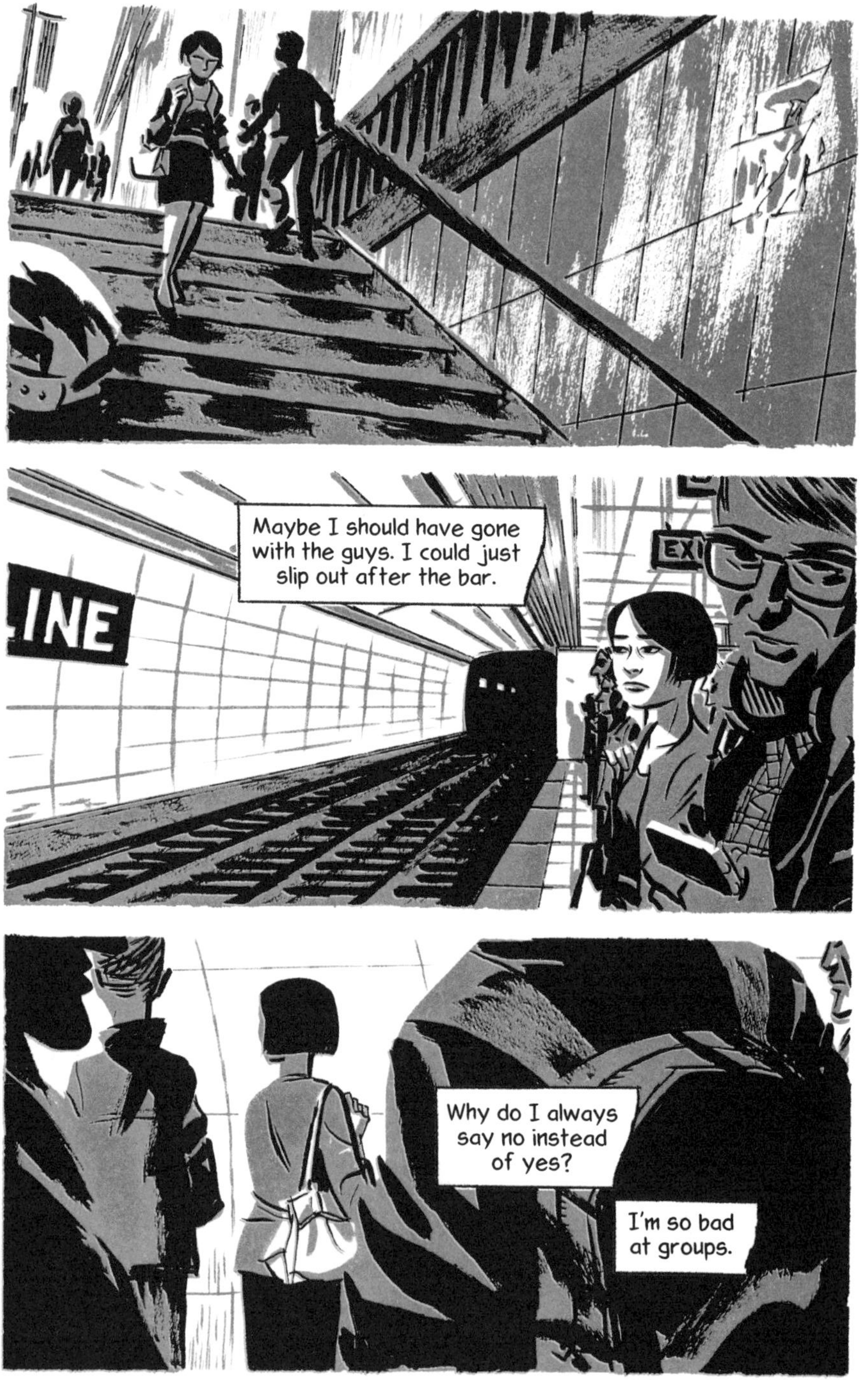
INE
EXI
Maybe I should have gone with the guys. I could just slip out after the bar.
Why do I always say no instead of yes?
I'm so bad at groups.

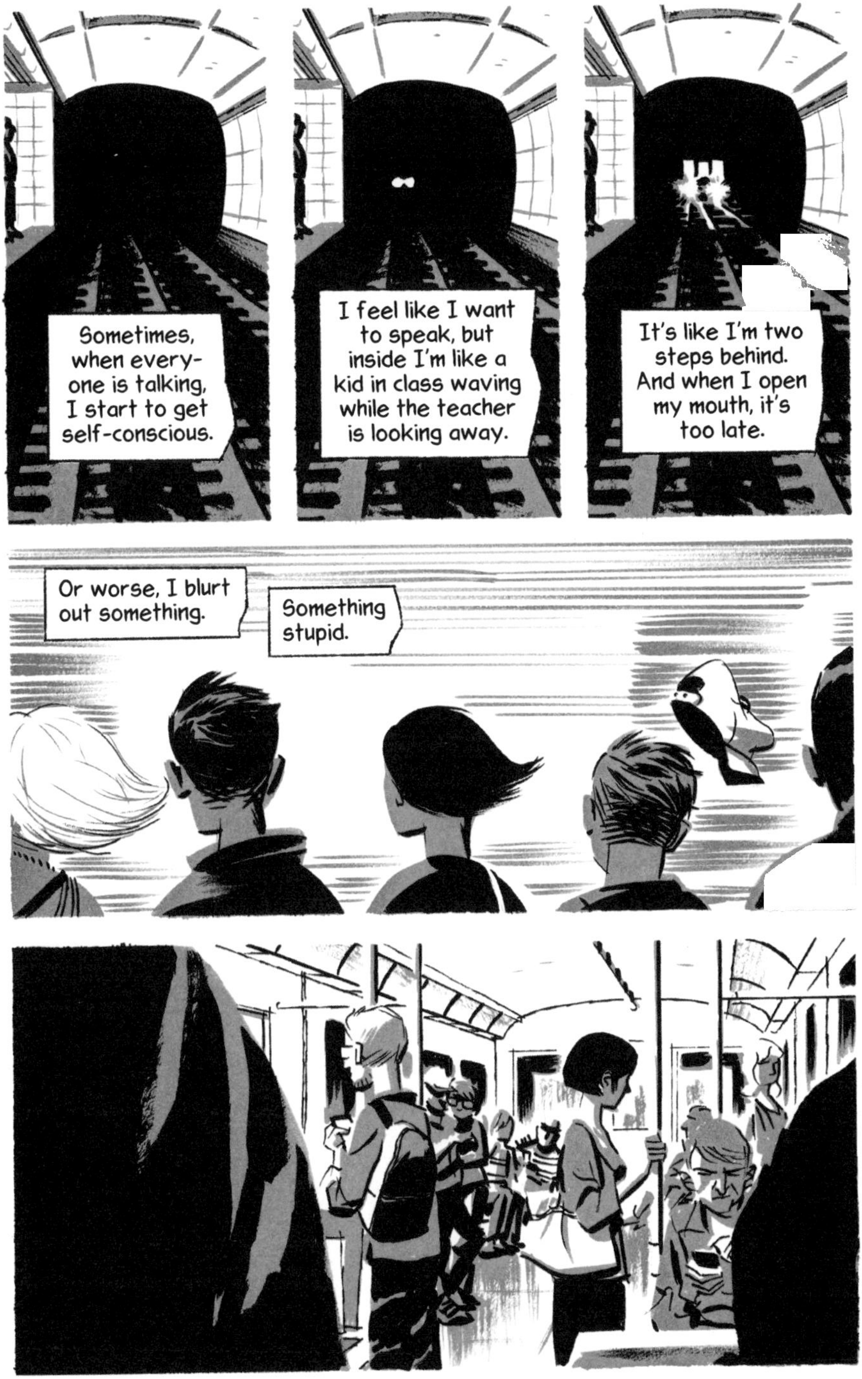
Sometimes, when every-one is talking, I start to get self-conscious.
I feel like I want to speak, but inside I'm like a kid in class waving while the teacher is looking away.
It's like I'm two steps behind. And when I open my mouth, it's too late.
Or worse, I blurt out something.
Something stupid.

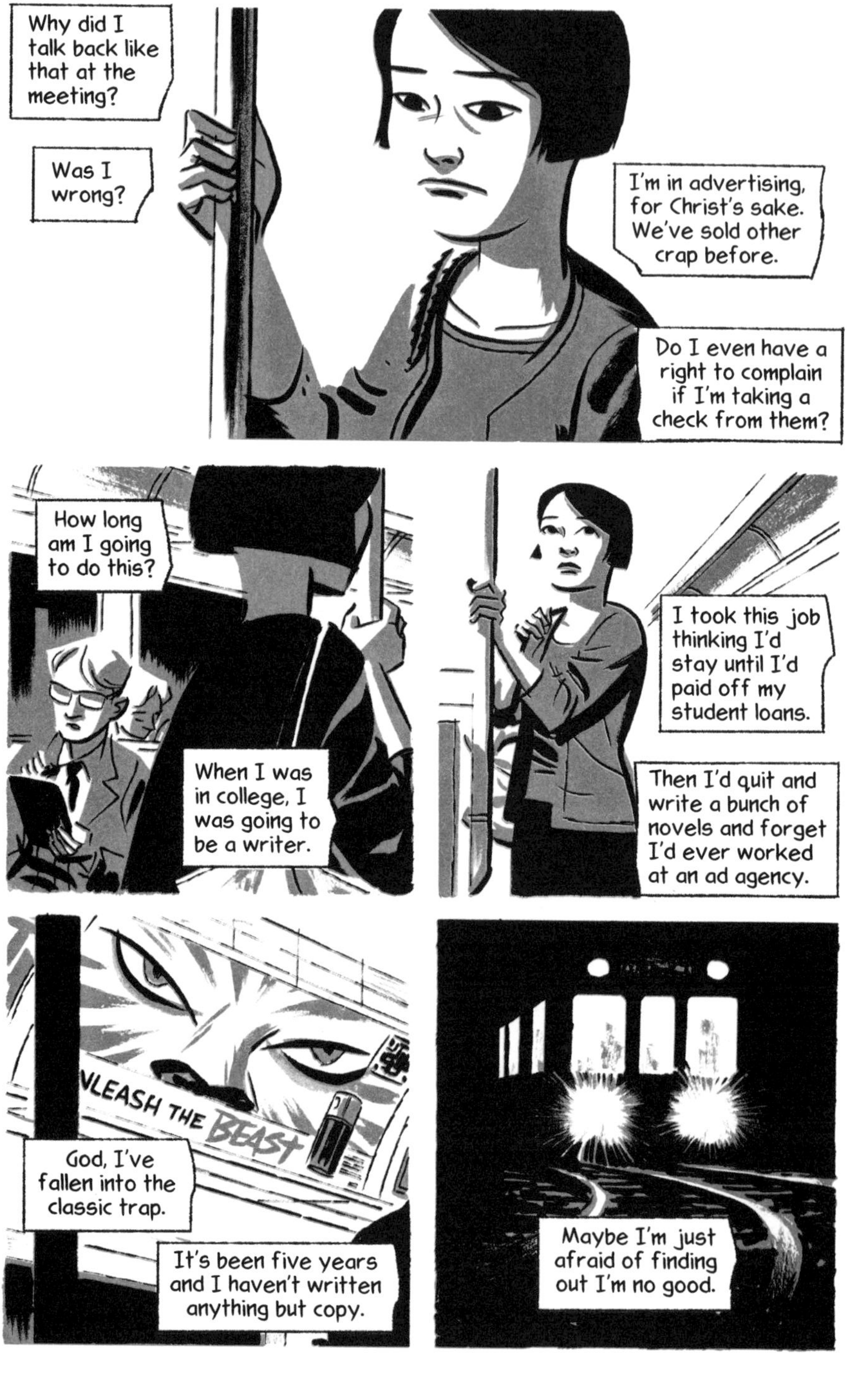
Why did I talk back like that at the meeting?
Was I wrong?
I'm in advertising, for Christ's sake. We've sold other crap before.
Do I even have a right to complain if I'm taking a check from them?
How long am I going to do this?
When I was in college, I was going to be a writer.
I took this job thinking I'd stay until I'd paid off my student loans.
Then I'd quit and write a bunch of novels and forget I'd ever worked at an ad agency.
NLEASH THE BEAST
God, I've fallen into the classic trap.
It's been five years and I haven't written anything but copy.
Maybe I'm just afraid of finding out I'm no good.

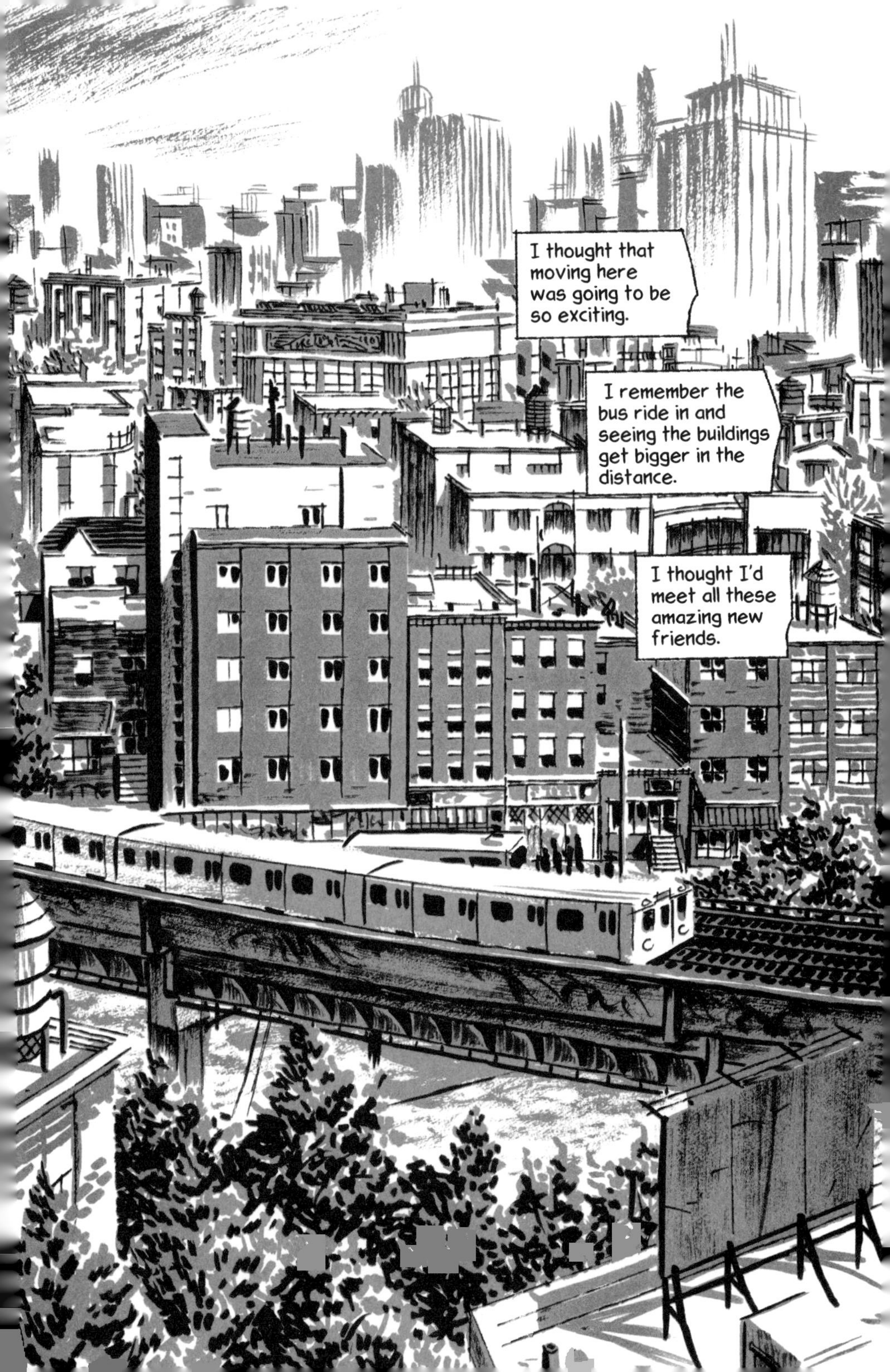
I thought that moving here was going to be so exciting.
I remember the bus ride in and seeing the buildings get bigger in the distance.
I thought I'd meet all these amazing new friends.

But I've been here for years now and I haven't really met anyone outside of work.

I used to visit my hometown friends once a month when I went back. But I was always catching up and outside the loop.

I wonder how many of them are married now?

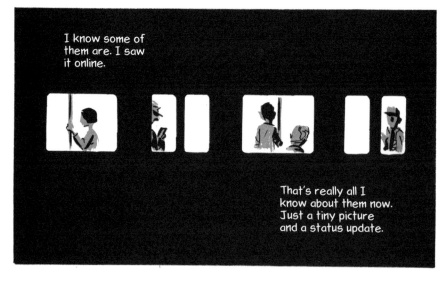

I know some of them are. I saw it online.

That's really all I know about them now. Just a tiny picture and a status update.

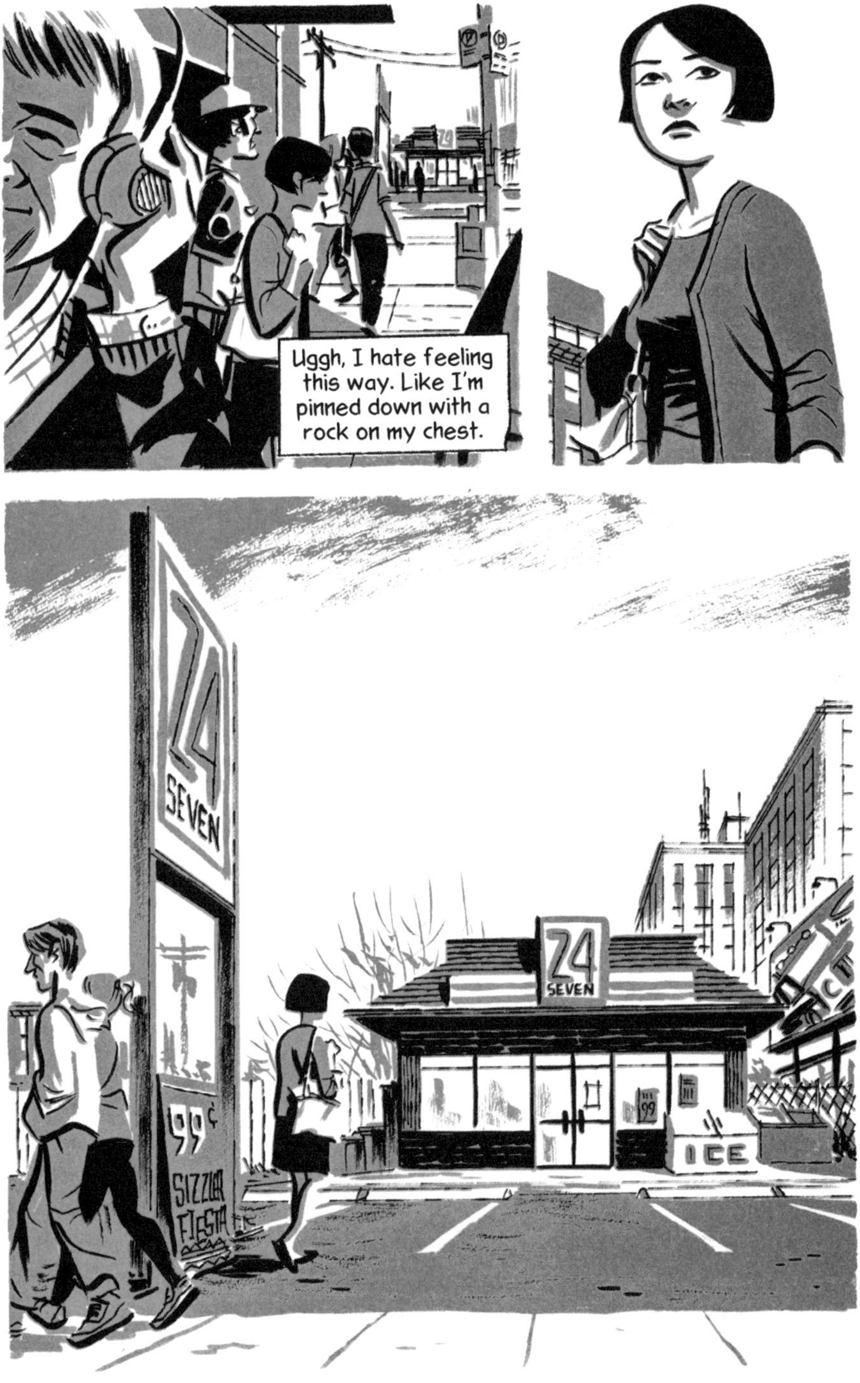
Uggh, I hate feeling this way. Like I'm pinned down with a rock on my chest.
24 SEVEN
99¢
SIZZLER FIESTA
24 SEVEN
ICE

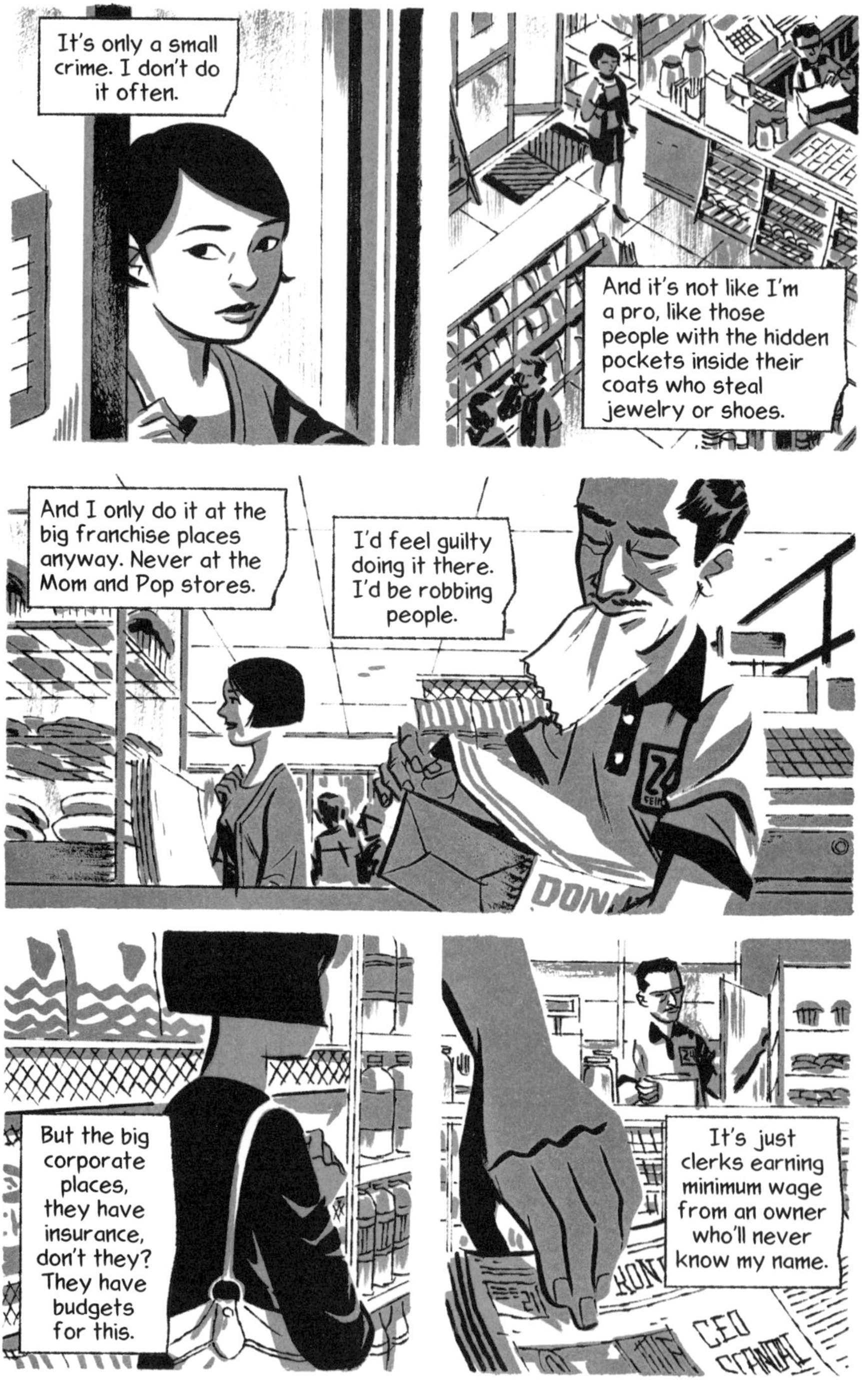

It's only a small crime. I don't do it often.
And it's not like I'm a pro, like those people with the hidden pockets inside their coats who steal jewelry or shoes.
And I only do it at the big franchise places anyway. Never at the Mom and Pop stores.
I'd feel guilty doing it there. I'd be robbing people.
But the big corporate places, they have insurance, don't they? They have budgets for this.
It's just clerks earning minimum wage from an owner who'll never know my name.
CEO SCANDAL

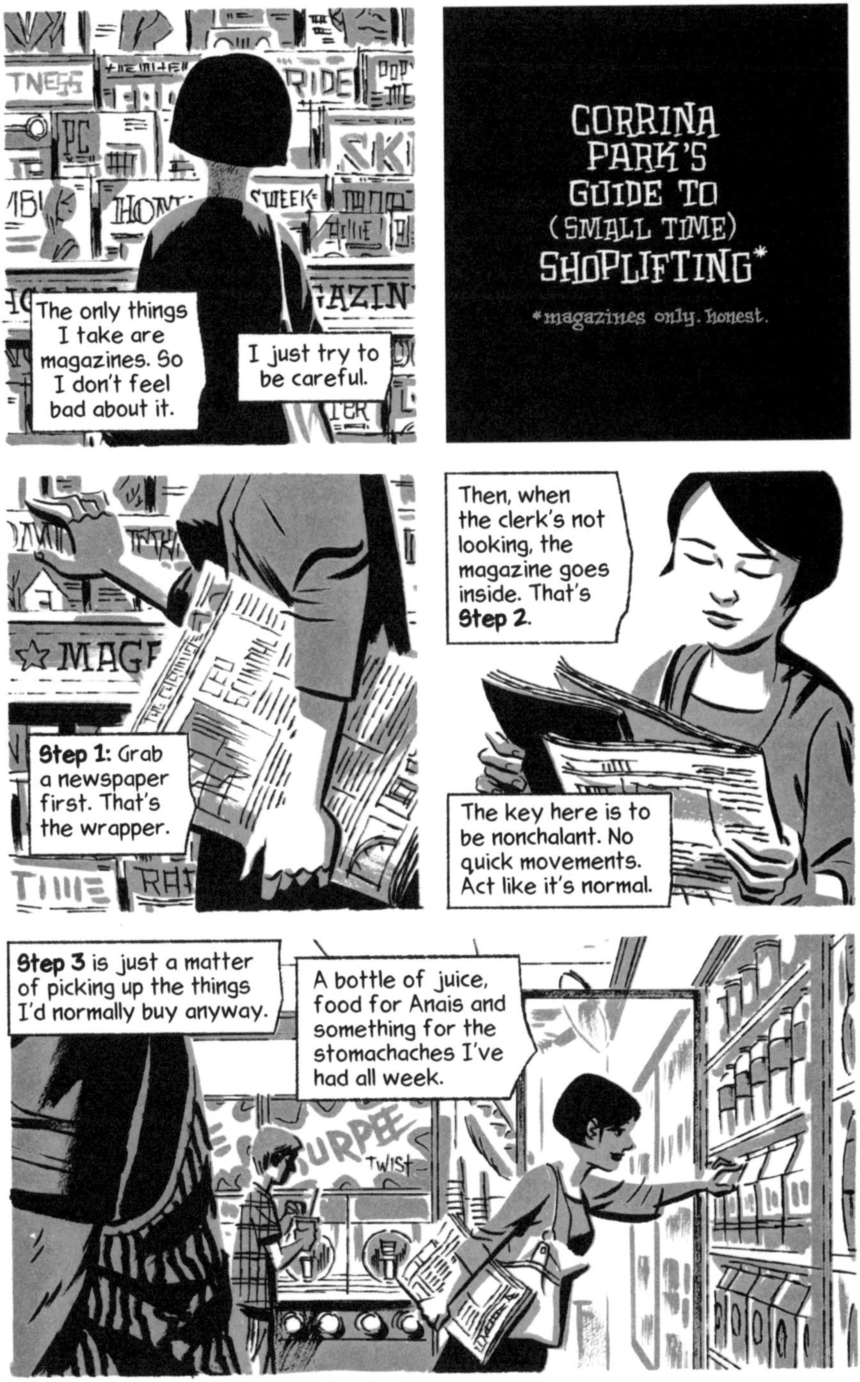
CORRINA PARK'S GUIDE TO (SMALL TIME) SHOPLIFTING*
*magazines only. honest.
The only things I take are magazines. So I don't feel bad about it.
I just try to be careful.
Step 1: Grab a newspaper first. That's the wrapper.
Then, when the clerk's not looking, the magazine goes inside. That's Step 2.
The key here is to be nonchalant. No quick movements. Act like it's normal.
Step 3 is just a matter of picking up the things I'd normally buy anyway.
A bottle of juice, food for Anais and something for the stomachaches I've had all week.
TWIST

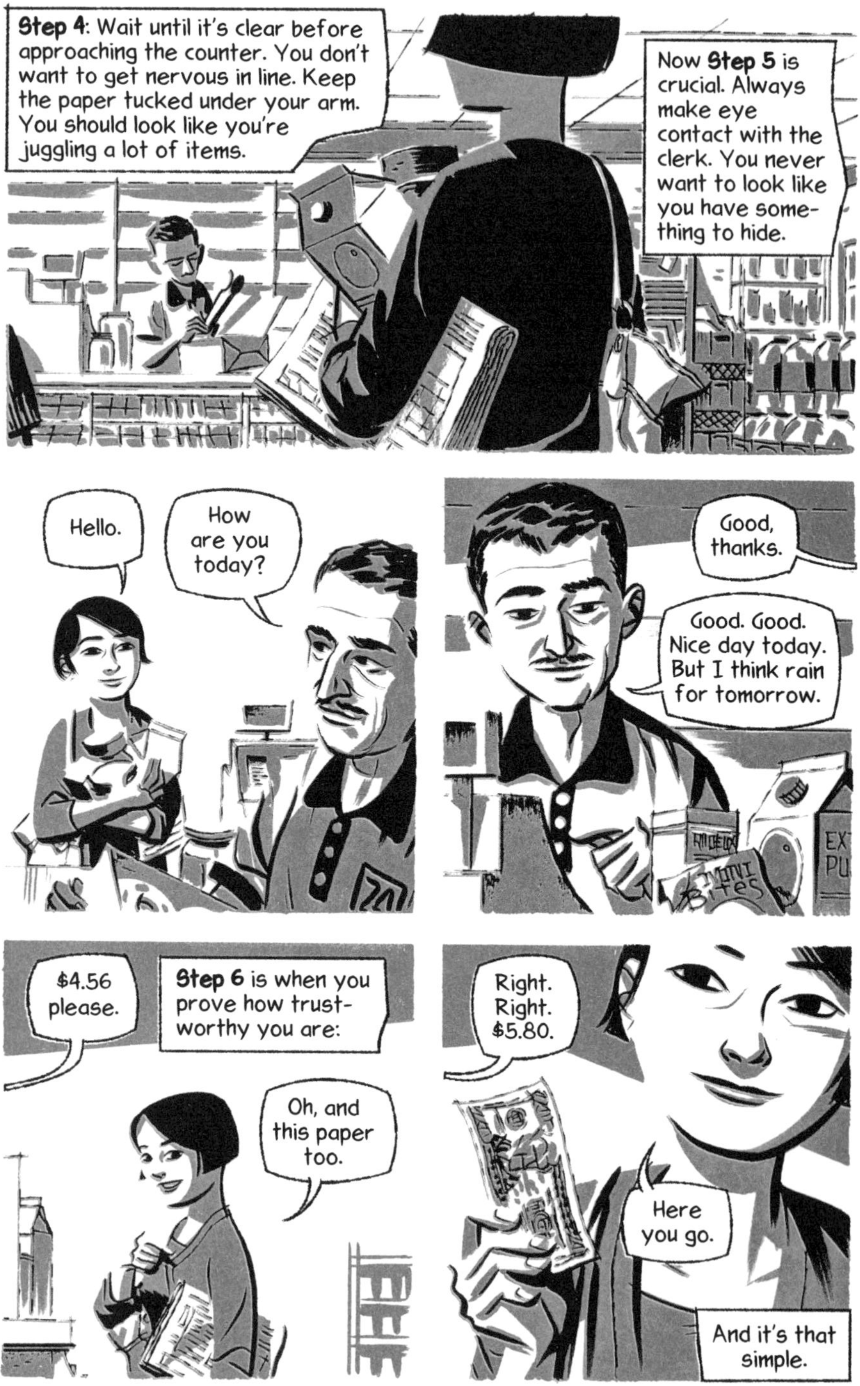
Step 4: Wait until it's clear before approaching the counter. You don't want to get nervous in line. Keep the paper tucked under your arm. You should look like you're juggling a lot of items.
Now Step 5 is crucial. Always make eye contact with the clerk. You never want to look like you have something to hide.
Hello.
How are you today?
Good, thanks.
Good. Good. Nice day today. But I think rain for tomorrow.
$4.56 please.
Step 6 is when you prove how trustworthy you are:
Oh, and this paper too.
Right. Right. $5.80.
Here you go.
And it's that simple.

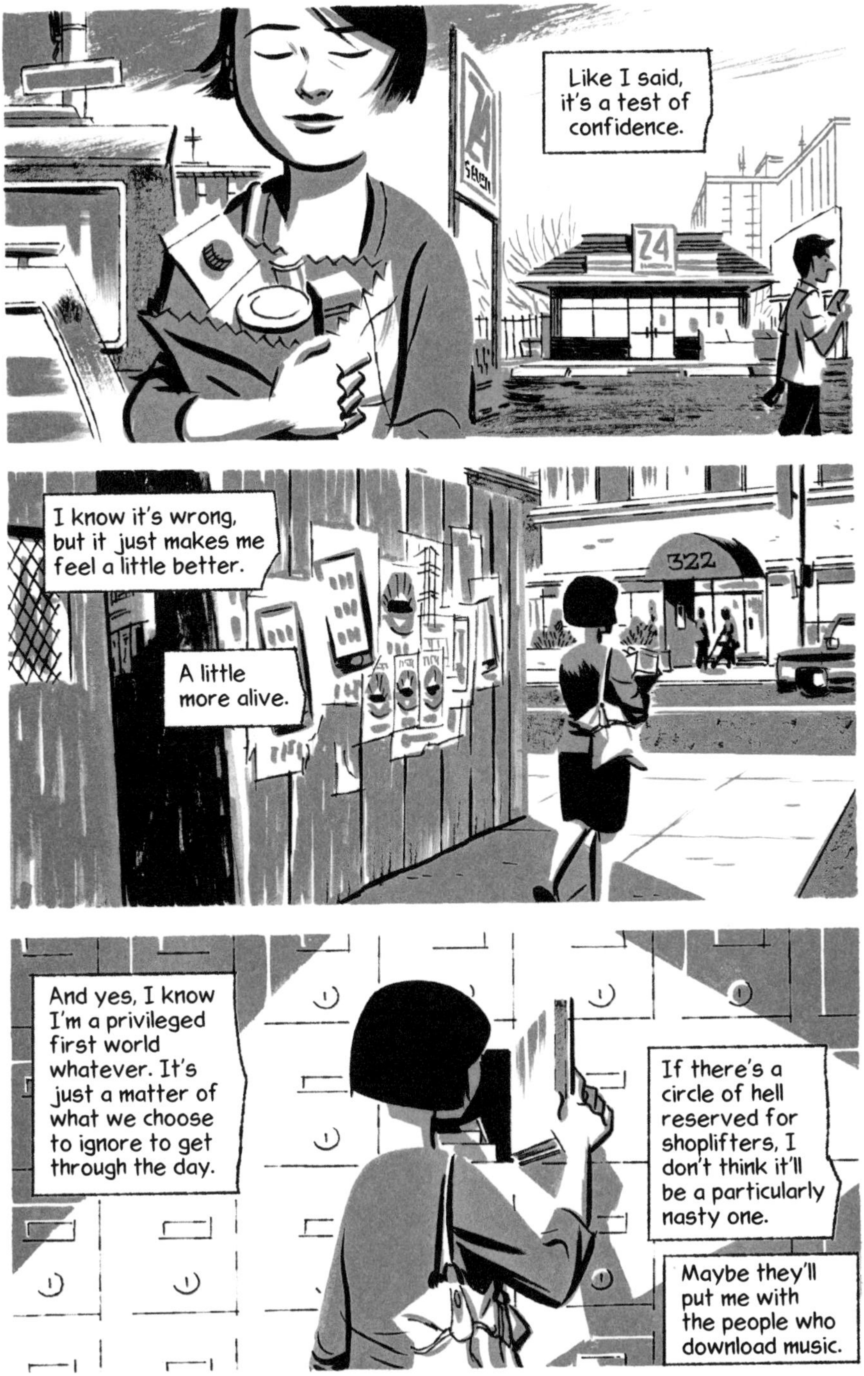
24
24
Like I said, it's a test of confidence.
I know it's wrong, but it just makes me feel a little better.
A little more alive.
322
And yes, I know I'm a privileged first world whatever. It's just a matter of what we choose to ignore to get through the day.
If there's a circle of hell reserved for shoplifters, I don't think it'll be a particularly nasty one.
Maybe they'll put me with the people who download music.

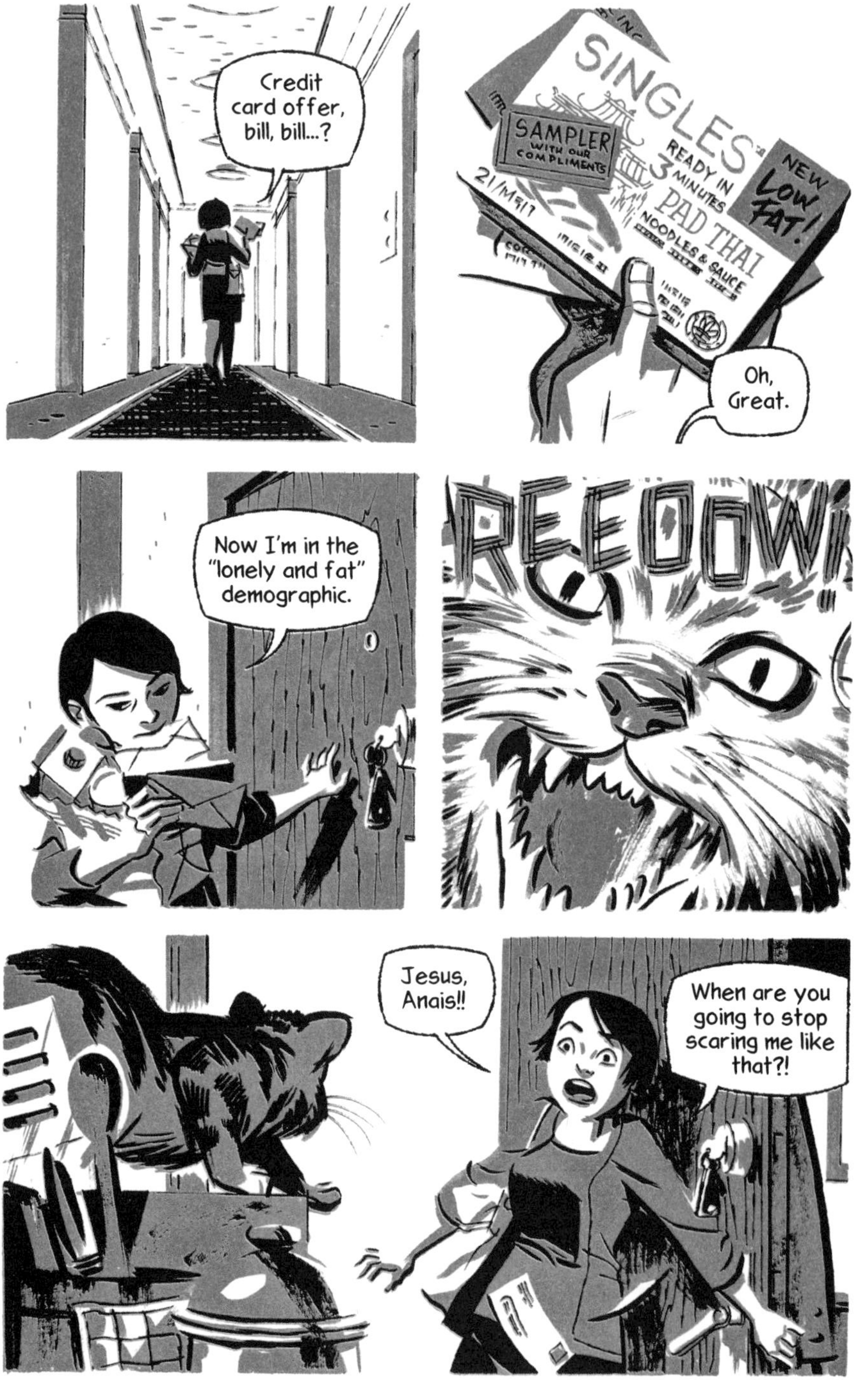
Credit card offer, bill, bill...?
SINGLES
SAMPLER WITH OUR COMPLIMENTS
READY IN 3 MINUTES
PAD THAI
NOODLES & SAUCE
NEW LOW FAT!
Oh, Great.
Now I'm in the "lonely and fat" demographic.
REEOOW
Jesus, Anais!!
When are you going to stop scaring me like that?!

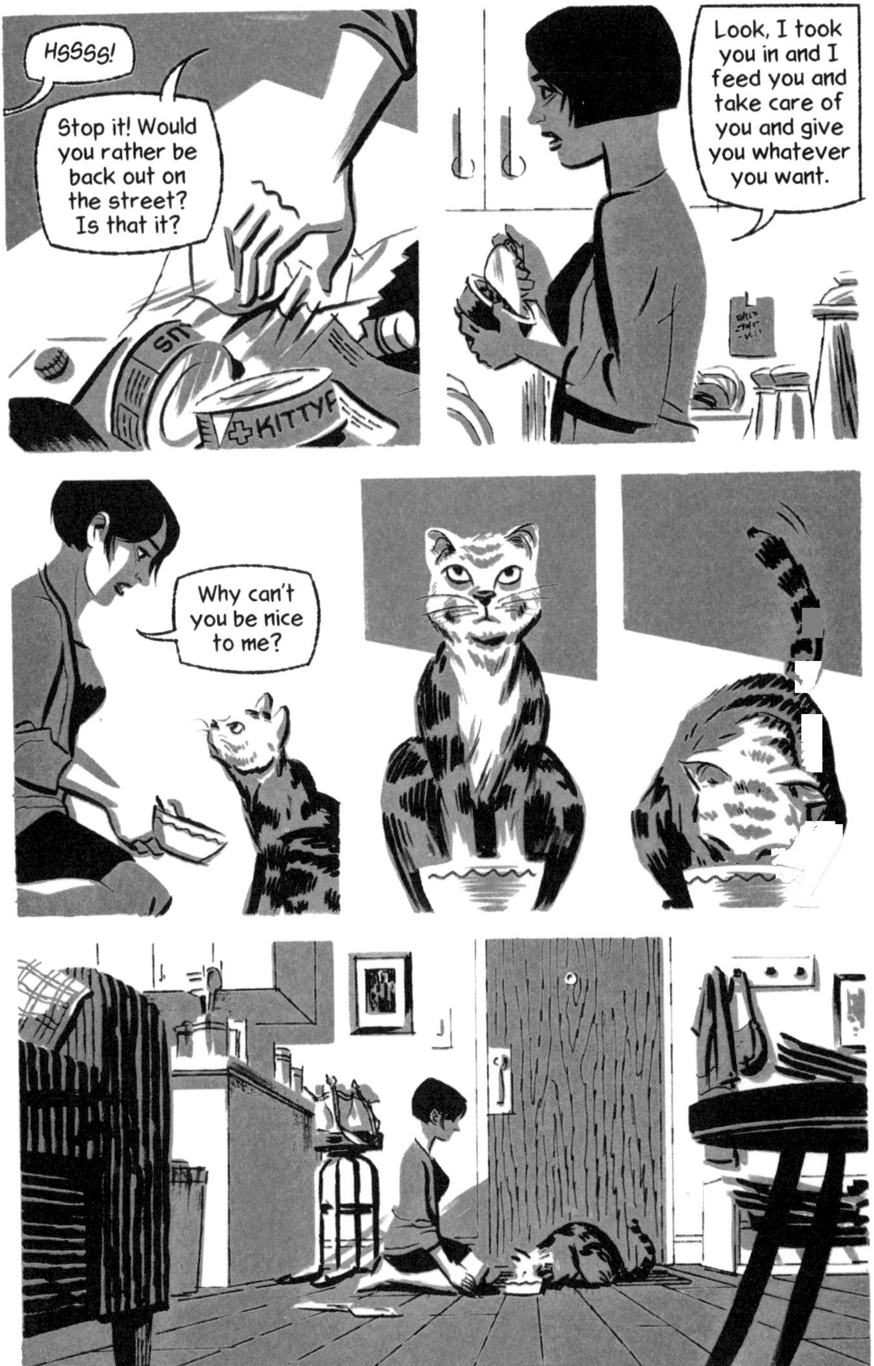
HSSSS!
Stop it! Would you rather be back out on the street? Is that it?
KITTY
Look, I took you in and I feed you and take care of you and give you whatever you want.
Why can't you be nice to me?

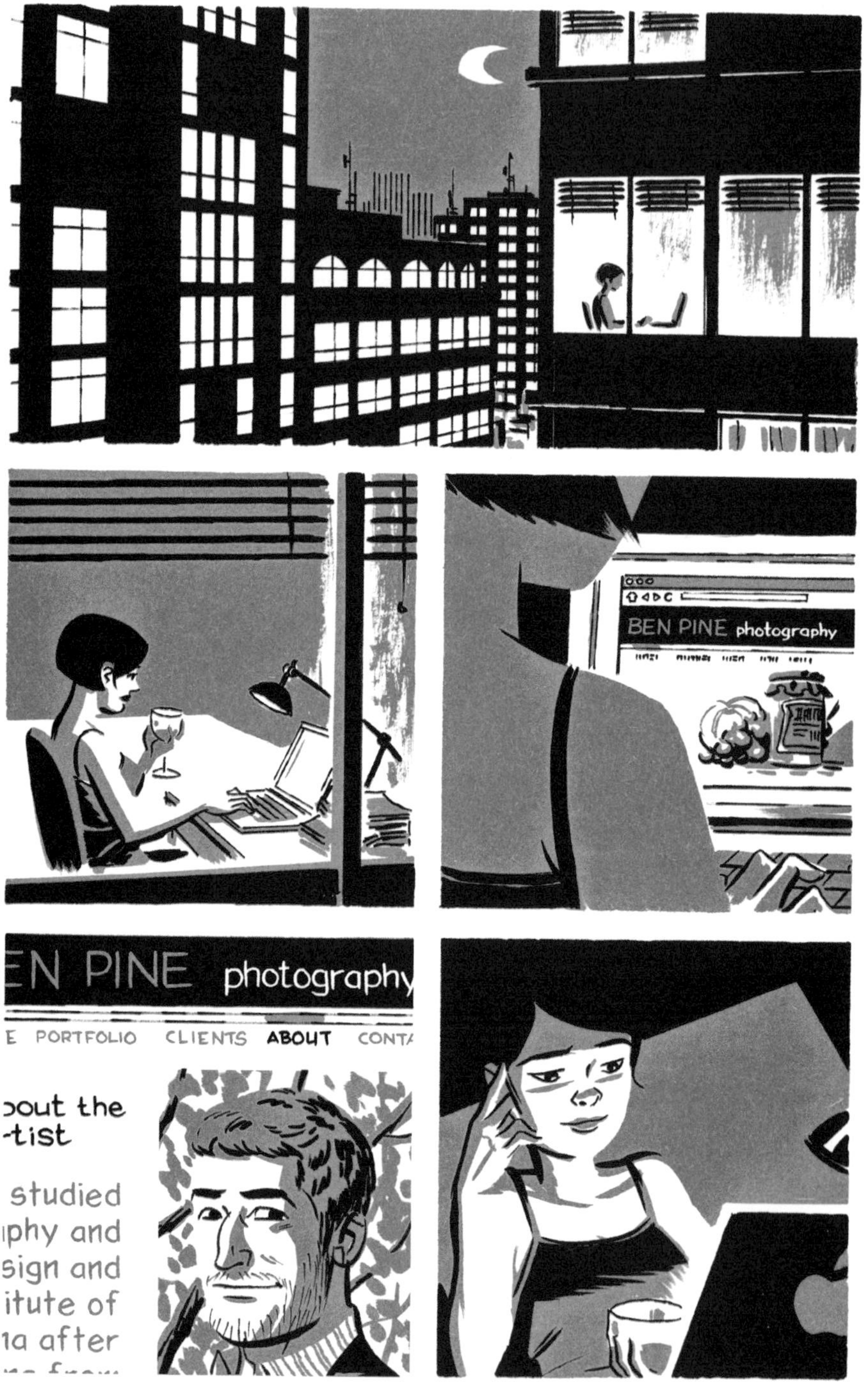

BEN PINE photography
EN PINE photography
PORTFOLIO CLIENTS ABOUT
studied
phy and
sign and
itute of
a after

CLICK! TAP TAP

CUPID*life*

LOGIN

TAP
TAP
TAP

CUPID*life*

Welcome back,
**virginiawoof**

Since your last log
5 people *PEEPED* ⸱
1 person *WINKED*

To read unread cli
Send a smile to ar

CLICK!

♡ ☒

from: mastrblastr
FREQUENT VISITOR

26 m here. I like ur
profile. IM me 4 hot
chat or rp. Cam 2
cam.

Also: feet pix?

CLICK

♡ ☒

from: hawkwinder 👍
VERIFIED MEMBER

From your profile, I
can tell that you are
a sensual librarian. I
want to give you an
extraordinary gift:
the gift of beautiful,
loving sex with an
attentive CLICK

♡ ☒

from: bl26-5kyd6 ⊕
NEW MEMBER

Buy effexor. Buy
effexor online. Also
xanax, oxycontin.
All brands.

CLICK

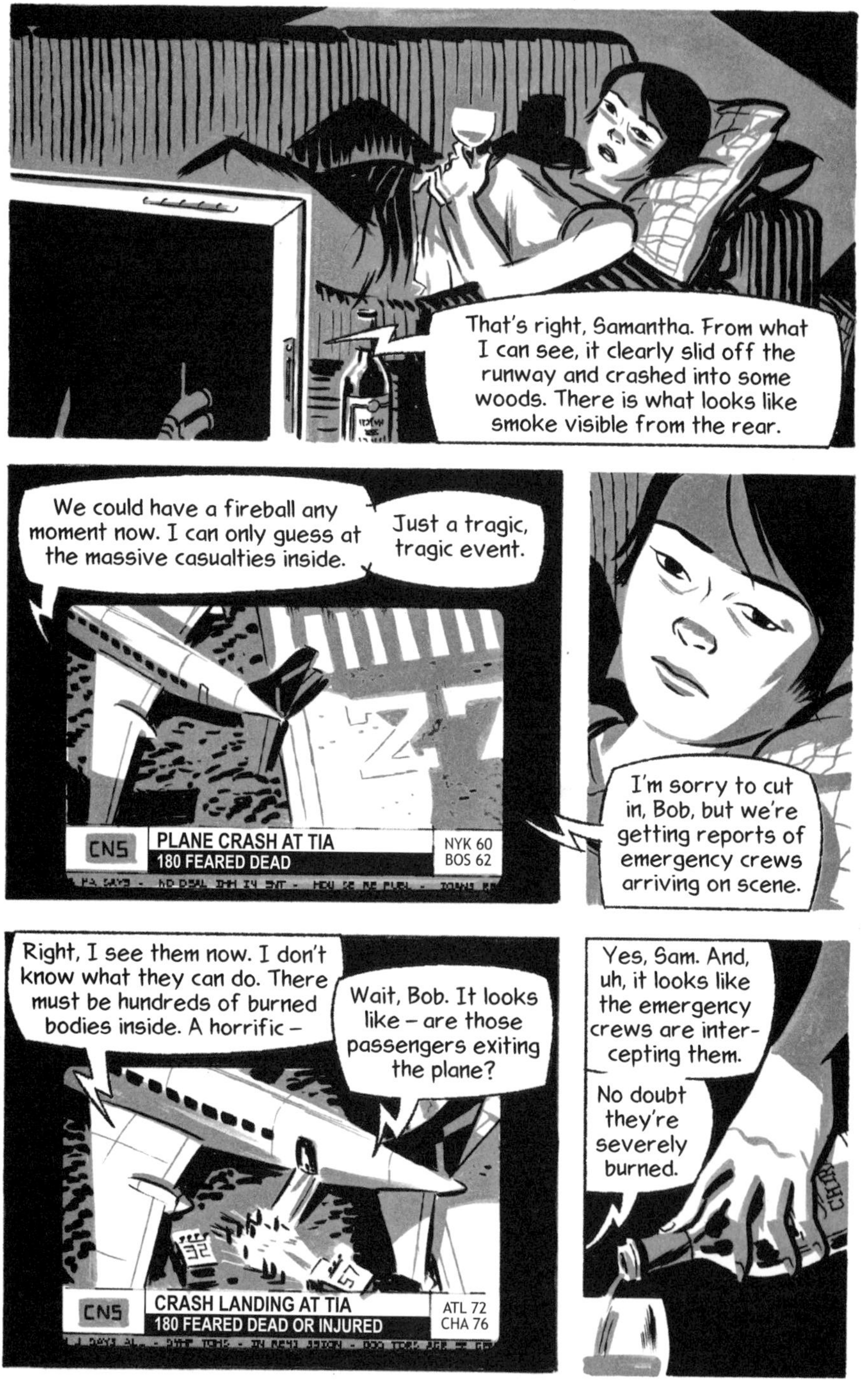

That's right, Samantha. From what I can see, it clearly slid off the runway and crashed into some woods. There is what looks like smoke visible from the rear.
We could have a fireball any moment now. I can only guess at the massive casualties inside.
Just a tragic, tragic event.
CNS
PLANE CRASH AT TIA
180 FEARED DEAD
NYK 60
BOS 62
I'm sorry to cut in, Bob, but we're getting reports of emergency crews arriving on scene.
Right, I see them now. I don't know what they can do. There must be hundreds of burned bodies inside. A horrific –
Wait, Bob. It looks like – are those passengers exiting the plane?
CNS
CRASH LANDING AT TIA
180 FEARED DEAD OR INJURED
ATL 72
CHA 76
Yes, Sam. And, uh, it looks like the emergency crews are intercepting them.
No doubt they're severely burned.

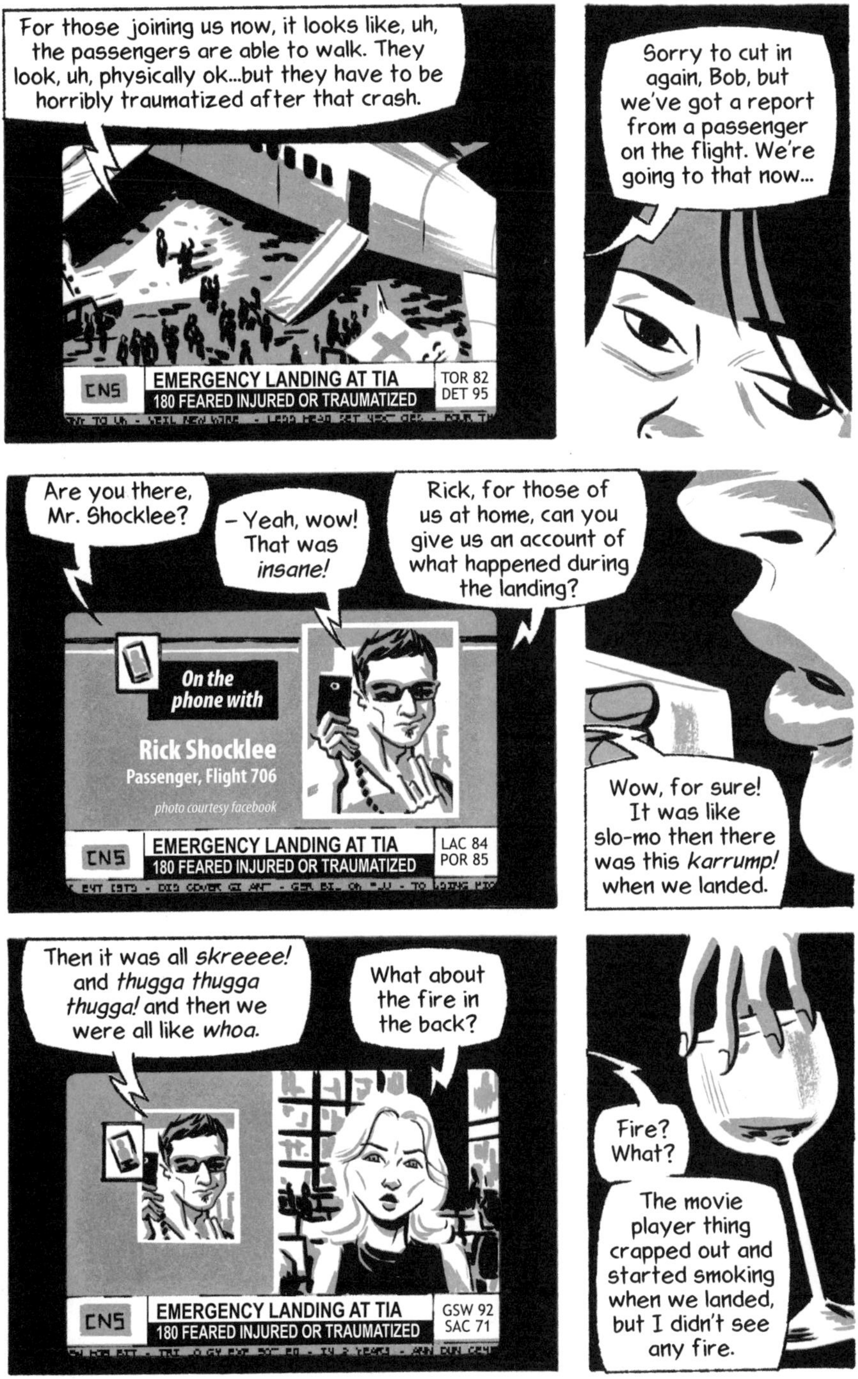
For those joining us now, it looks like, uh, the passengers are able to walk. They look, uh, physically ok...but they have to be horribly traumatized after that crash.
CNS
EMERGENCY LANDING AT TIA
180 FEARED INJURED OR TRAUMATIZED
TOR 82
DET 95
Sorry to cut in again, Bob, but we've got a report from a passenger on the flight. We're going to that now...
Are you there, Mr. Shocklee?
–Yeah, wow! That was *insane!*
Rick, for those of us at home, can you give us an account of what happened during the landing?
On the phone with
Rick Shocklee
Passenger, Flight 706
photo courtesy facebook
CNS
EMERGENCY LANDING AT TIA
180 FEARED INJURED OR TRAUMATIZED
LAC 84
POR 85
Wow, for sure! It was like slo-mo then there was this *karrump!* when we landed.
Then it was all *skreeee!* and *thugga thugga thugga!* and then we were all like *whoa.*
What about the fire in the back?
CNS
EMERGENCY LANDING AT TIA
180 FEARED INJURED OR TRAUMATIZED
GSW 92
SAC 71
Fire? What?
The movie player thing crapped out and started smoking when we landed, but I didn't see any fire.

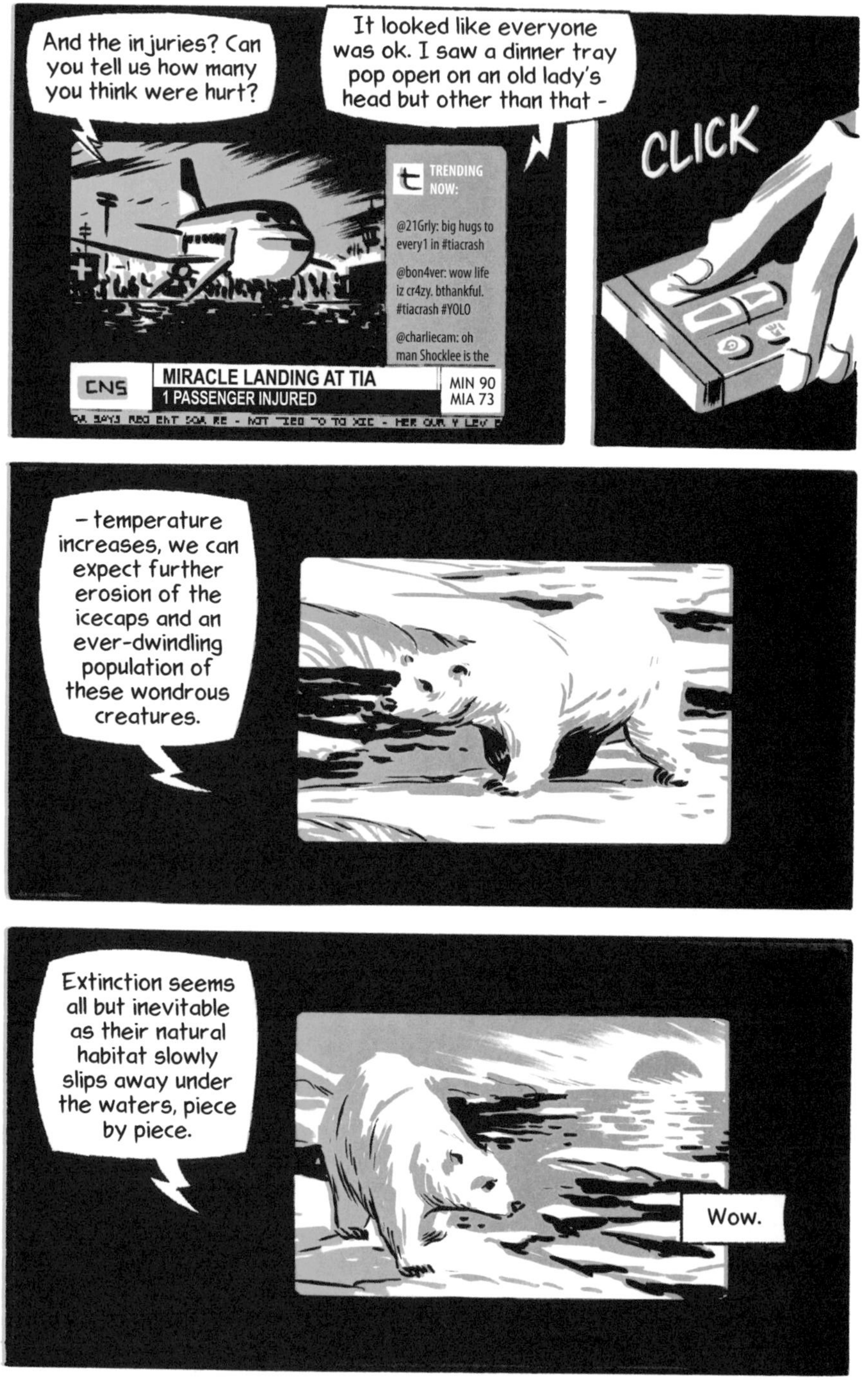

And the injuries? Can you tell us how many you think were hurt?
It looked like everyone was ok. I saw a dinner tray pop open on an old lady's head but other than that -
TRENDING NOW:
@21Grly: big hugs to every1 in #tiacrash
@bon4ver: wow life iz cr4zy. bthankful. #tiacrash #YOLO
@charliecam: oh man Shocklee is the
CNS
MIRACLE LANDING AT TIA
1 PASSENGER INJURED
MIN 90
MIA 73
CLICK
– temperature increases, we can expect further erosion of the icecaps and an ever-dwindling population of these wondrous creatures.
Extinction seems all but inevitable as their natural habitat slowly slips away under the waters, piece by piece.
Wow.

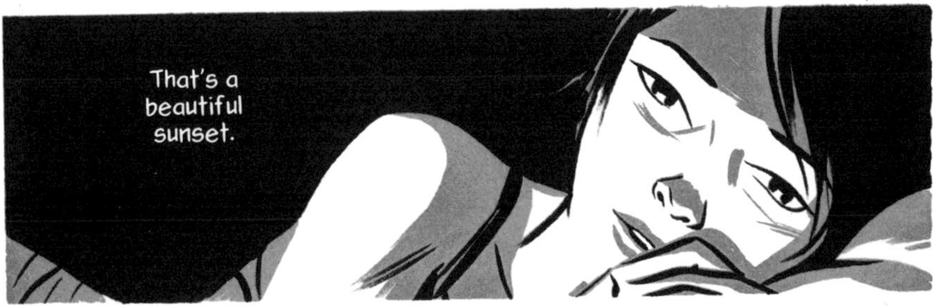
That's a beautiful sunset.

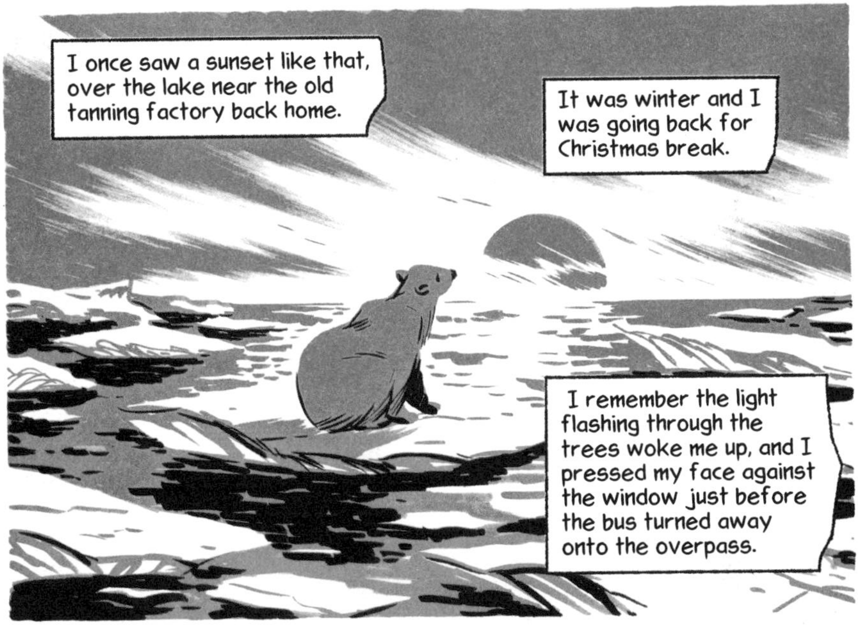
I once saw a sunset like that, over the lake near the old tanning factory back home.
It was winter and I was going back for Christmas break.
I remember the light flashing through the trees woke me up, and I pressed my face against the window just before the bus turned away onto the overpass.

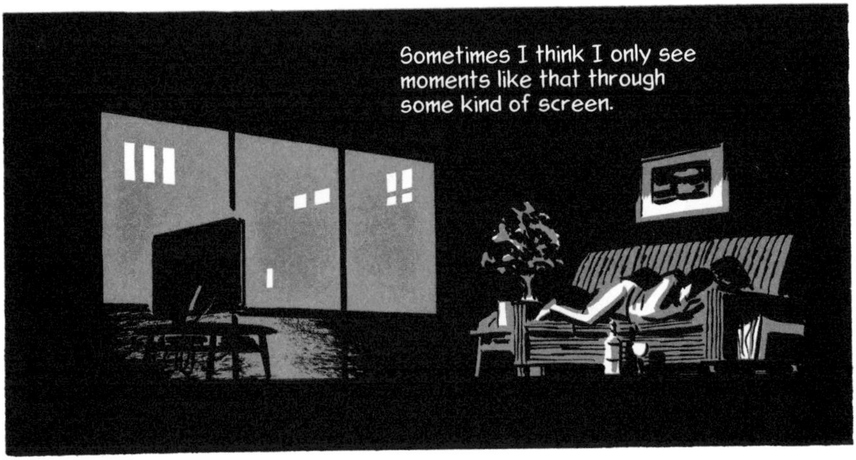
Sometimes I think I only see moments like that through some kind of screen.

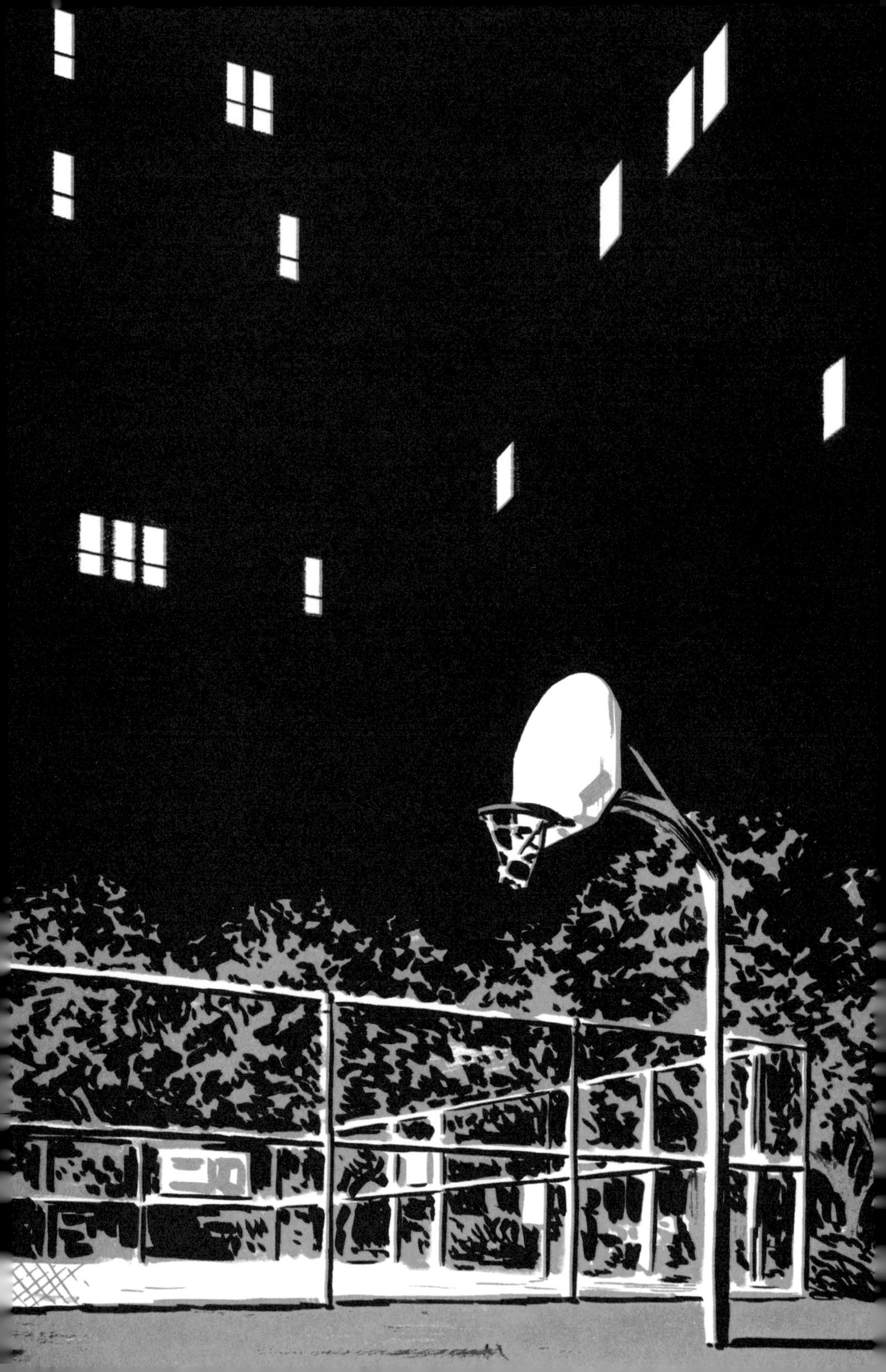

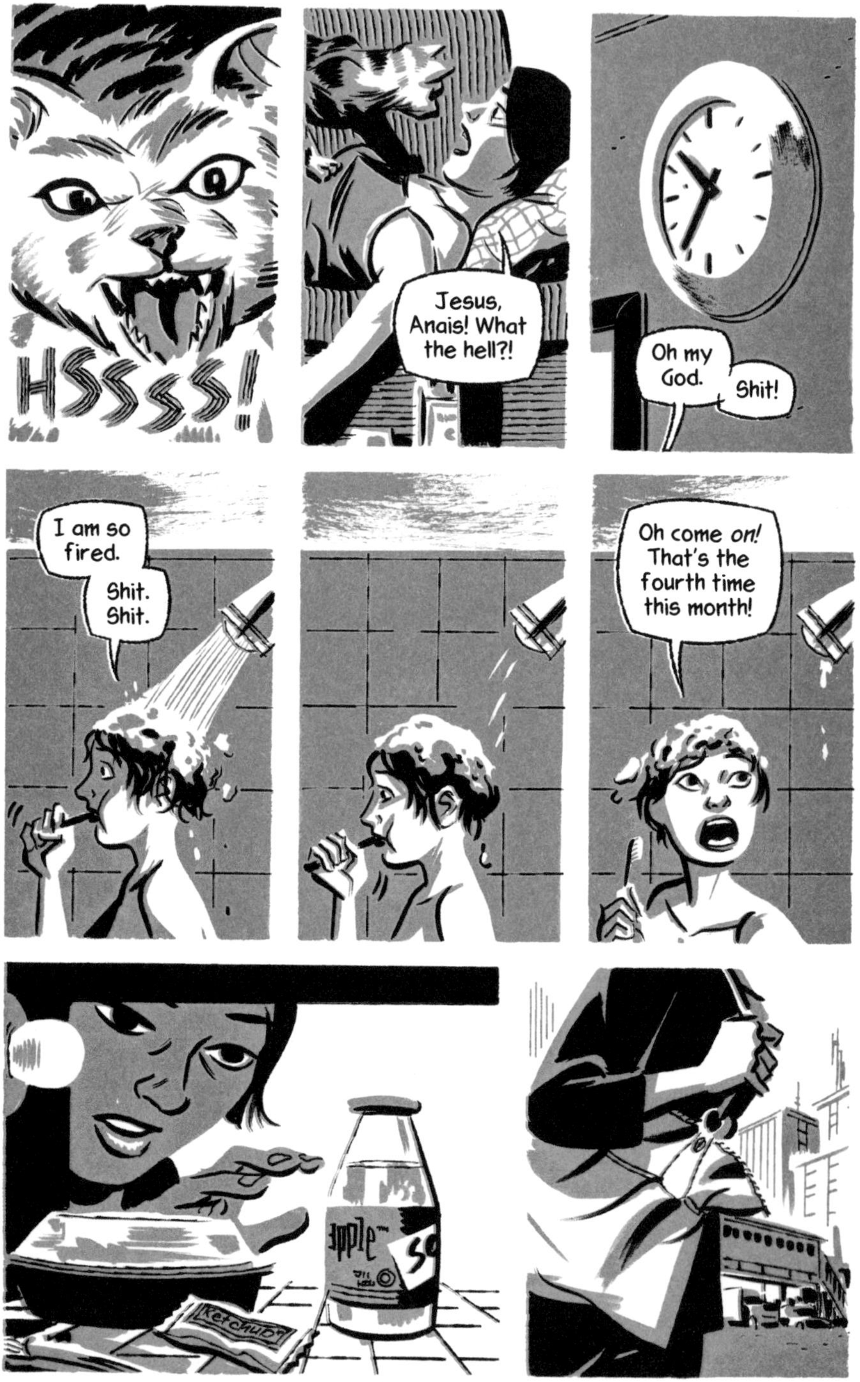
HSSSS!
Jesus, Anais! What the hell?!
Oh my God.
Shit!
I am so fired.
Shit. Shit.
Oh come *on!* That's the fourth time this month!
apple
Ketchup

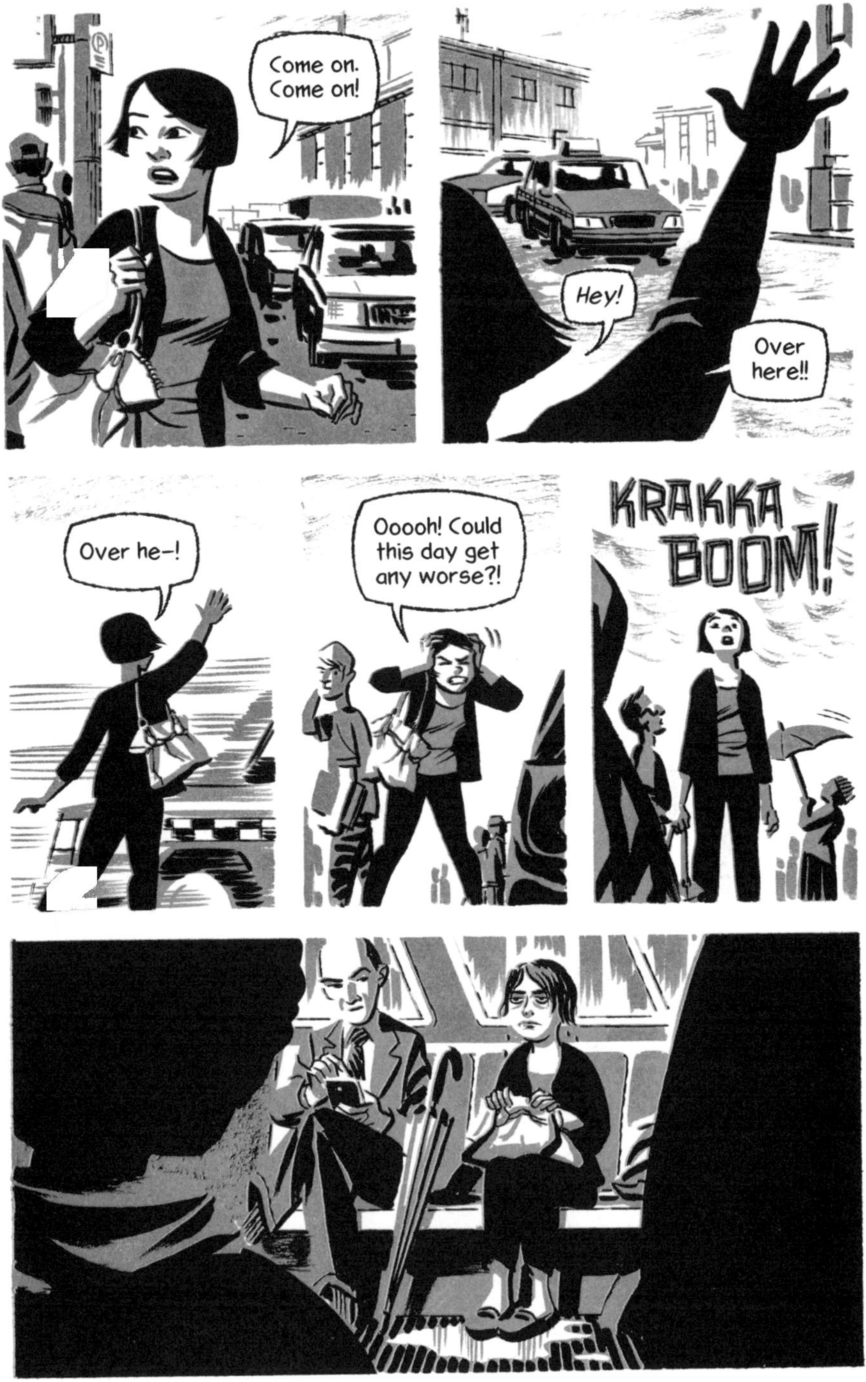
Come on.
Come on!
Hey!
Over here!!
Over he-!
Ooooh! Could this day get any worse?!
KRAKKA BOOM!

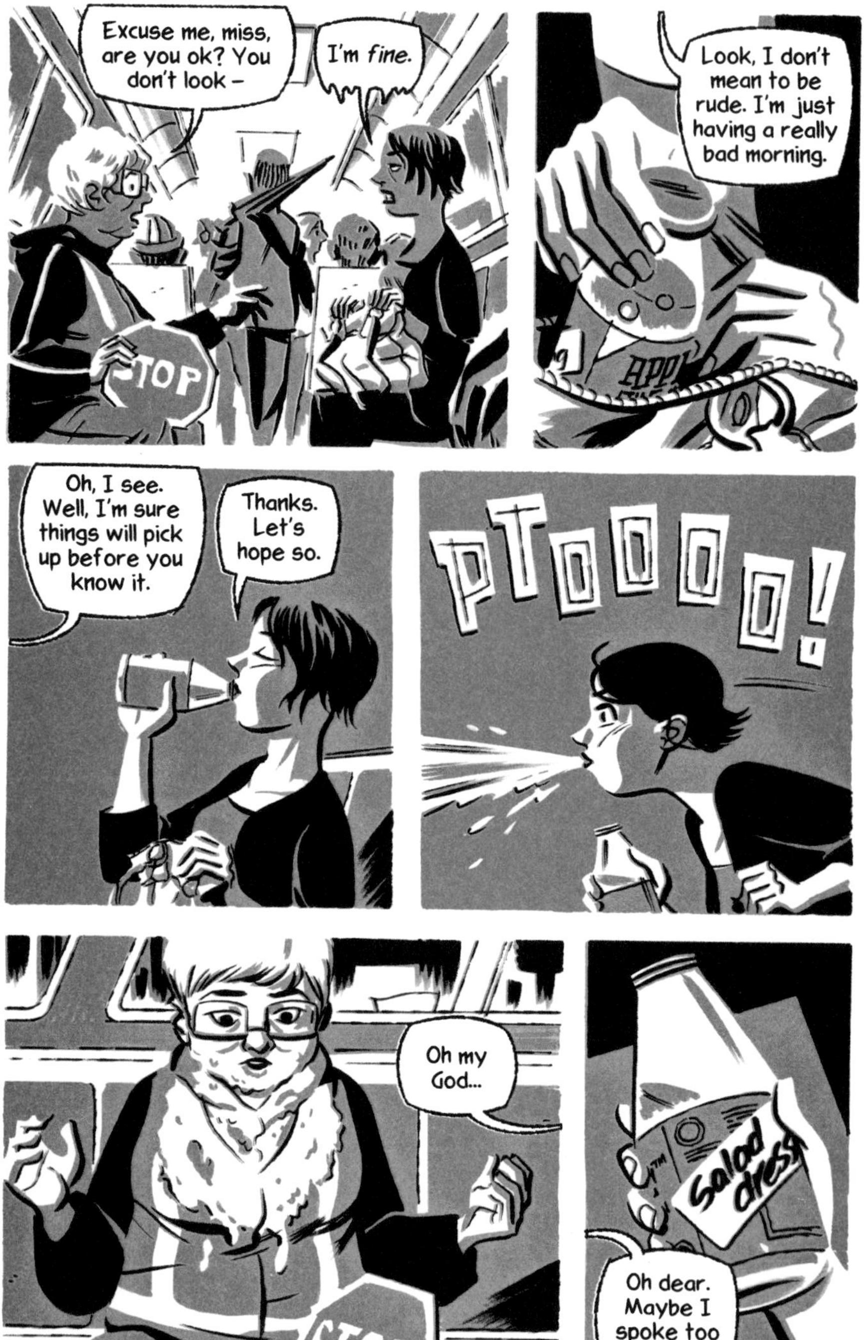
Excuse me, miss, are you ok? You don't look –
I'm *fine.*
Look, I don't mean to be rude. I'm just having a really bad morning.
Oh, I see. Well, I'm sure things will pick up before you know it.
Thanks. Let's hope so.
PTOOOO!
Oh my God...
Oh dear. Maybe I spoke too soon.
STOP

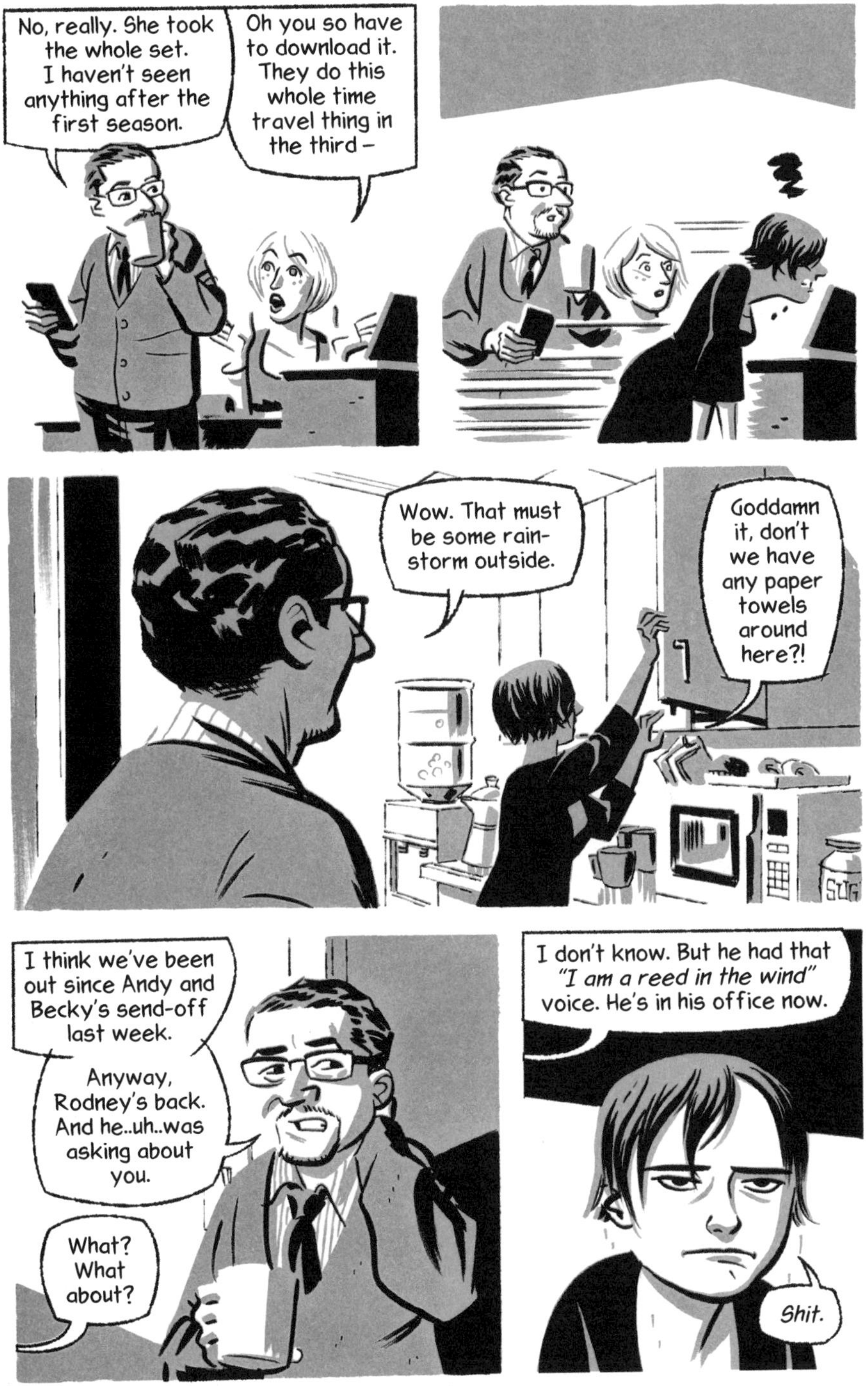
No, really. She took the whole set. I haven't seen anything after the first season.
Oh you so have to download it. They do this whole time travel thing in the third –
Wow. That must be some rain-storm outside.
Goddamn it, don't we have any paper towels around here?!
I think we've been out since Andy and Becky's send-off last week.
Anyway, Rodney's back. And he..uh..was asking about you.
What? What about?
I don't know. But he had that *"I am a reed in the wind"* voice. He's in his office now.
*Shit.*

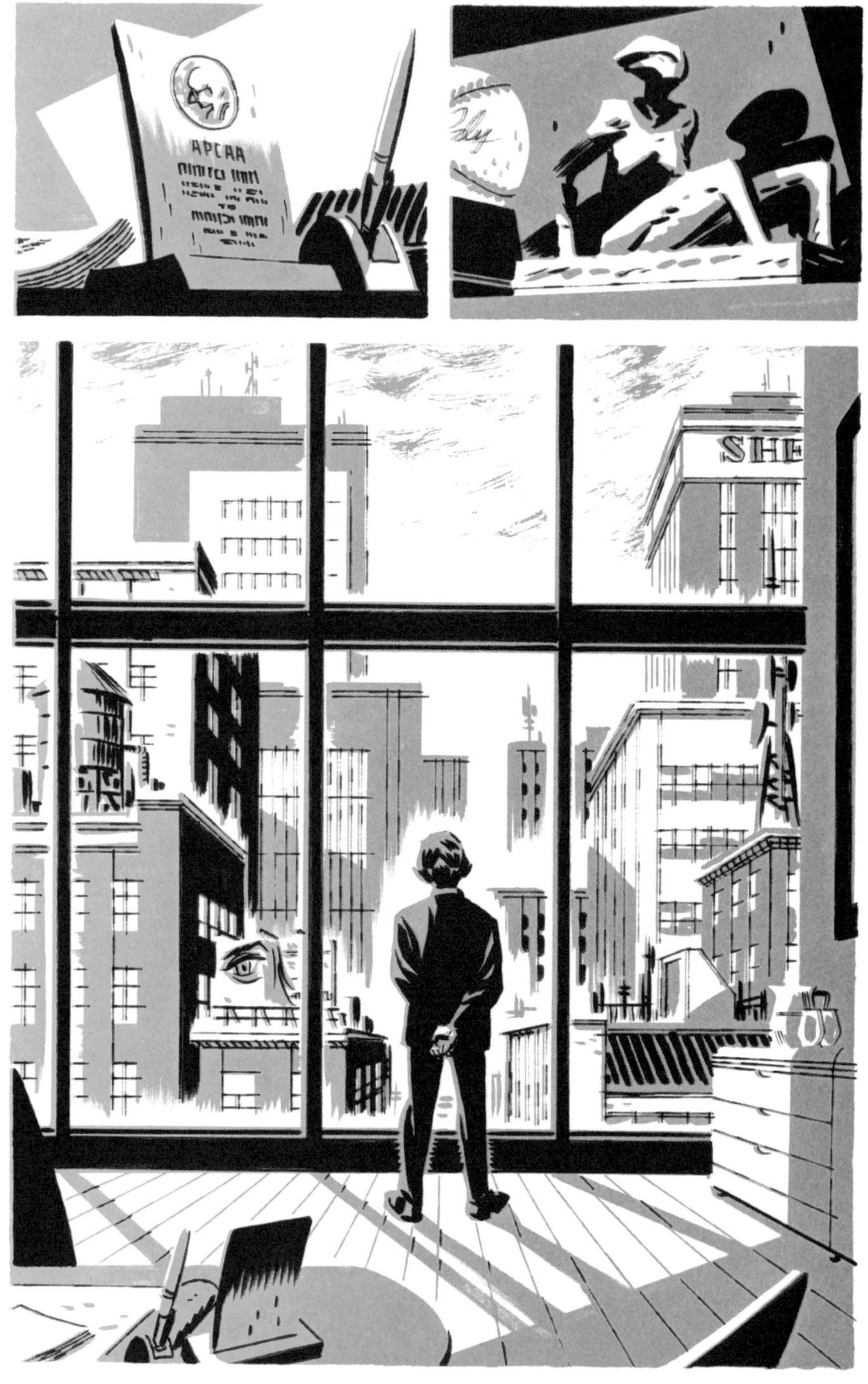
APCAA
SHE

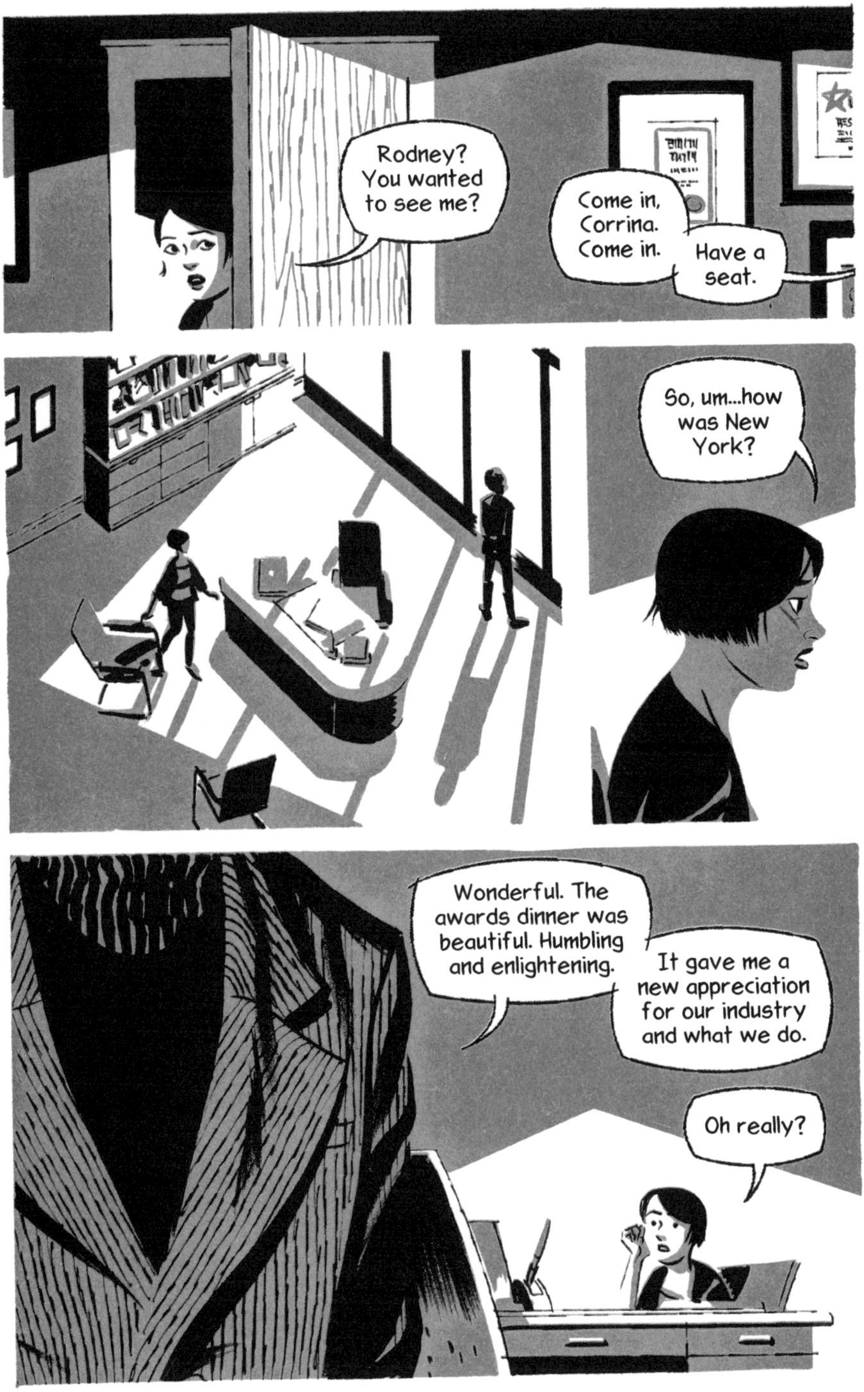
Rodney? You wanted to see me?
Come in, Corrina. Come in.
Have a seat.
So, um...how was New York?
Wonderful. The awards dinner was beautiful. Humbling and enlightening.
It gave me a new appreciation for our industry and what we do.
Oh really?

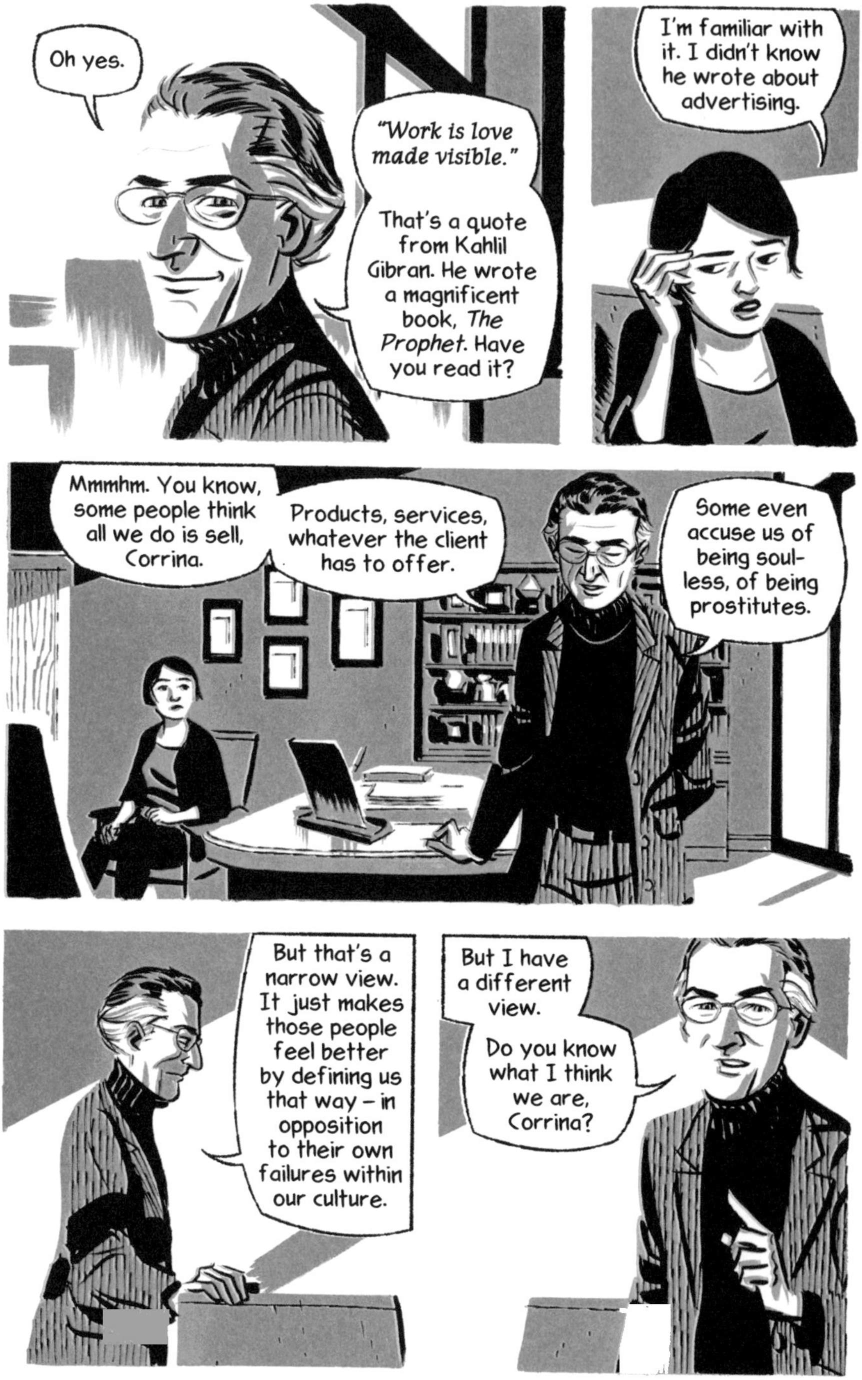
Oh yes.
"*Work is love made visible.*"
That's a quote from Kahlil Gibran. He wrote a magnificent book, *The Prophet*. Have you read it?
I'm familiar with it. I didn't know he wrote about advertising.
Mmmhm. You know, some people think all we do is sell, Corrina.
Products, services, whatever the client has to offer.
Some even accuse us of being soul-less, of being prostitutes.
But that's a narrow view. It just makes those people feel better by defining us that way – in opposition to their own failures within our culture.
But I have a different view.
Do you know what I think we are, Corrina?

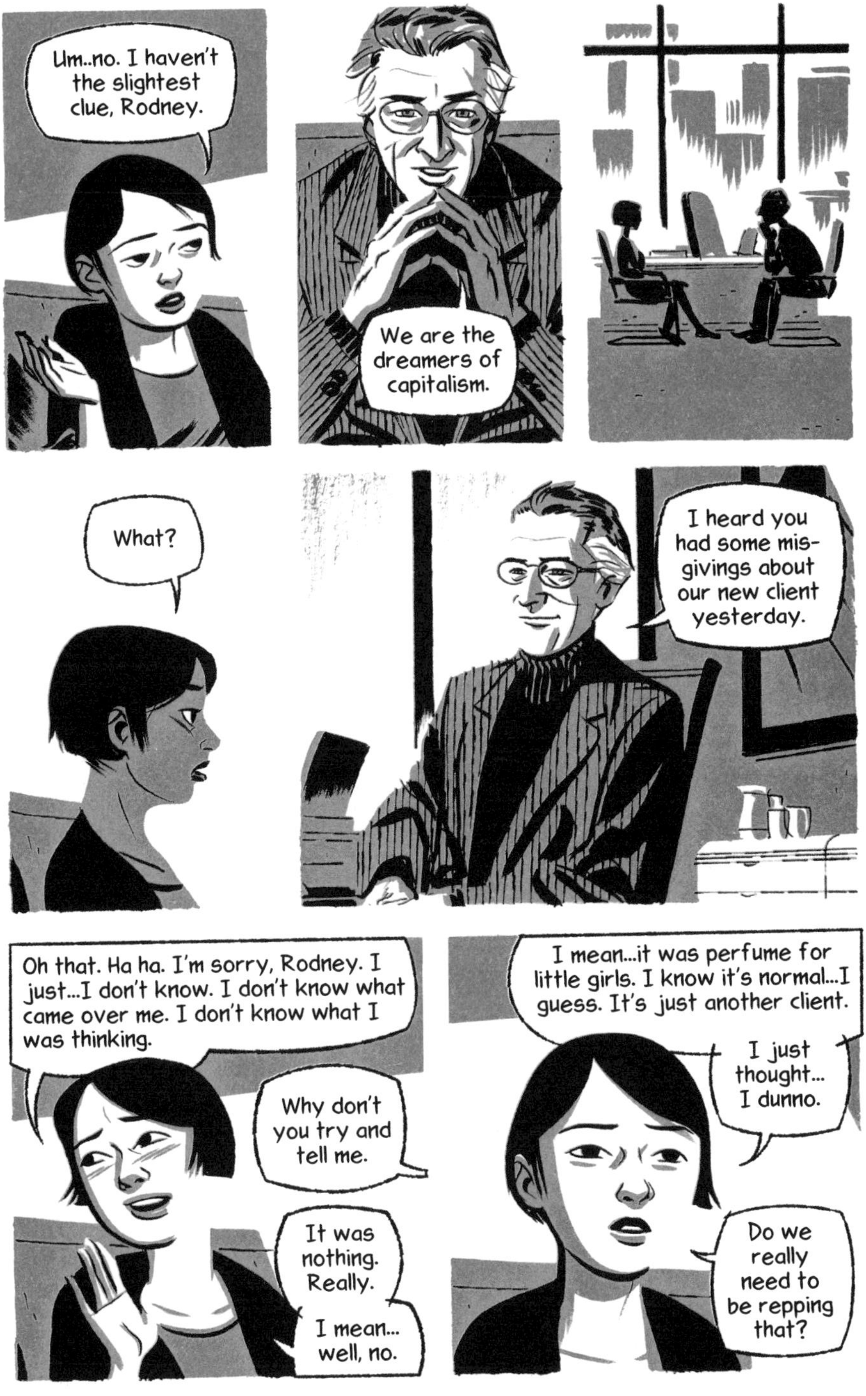

Um..no. I haven't the slightest clue, Rodney.
We are the dreamers of capitalism.
What?
I heard you had some mis-givings about our new client yesterday.
Oh that. Ha ha. I'm sorry, Rodney. I just...I don't know. I don't know what came over me. I don't know what I was thinking.
Why don't you try and tell me.
It was nothing. Really.
I mean... well, no.
I mean...it was perfume for little girls. I know it's normal...I guess. It's just another client.
I just thought... I dunno.
Do we really need to be repping that?

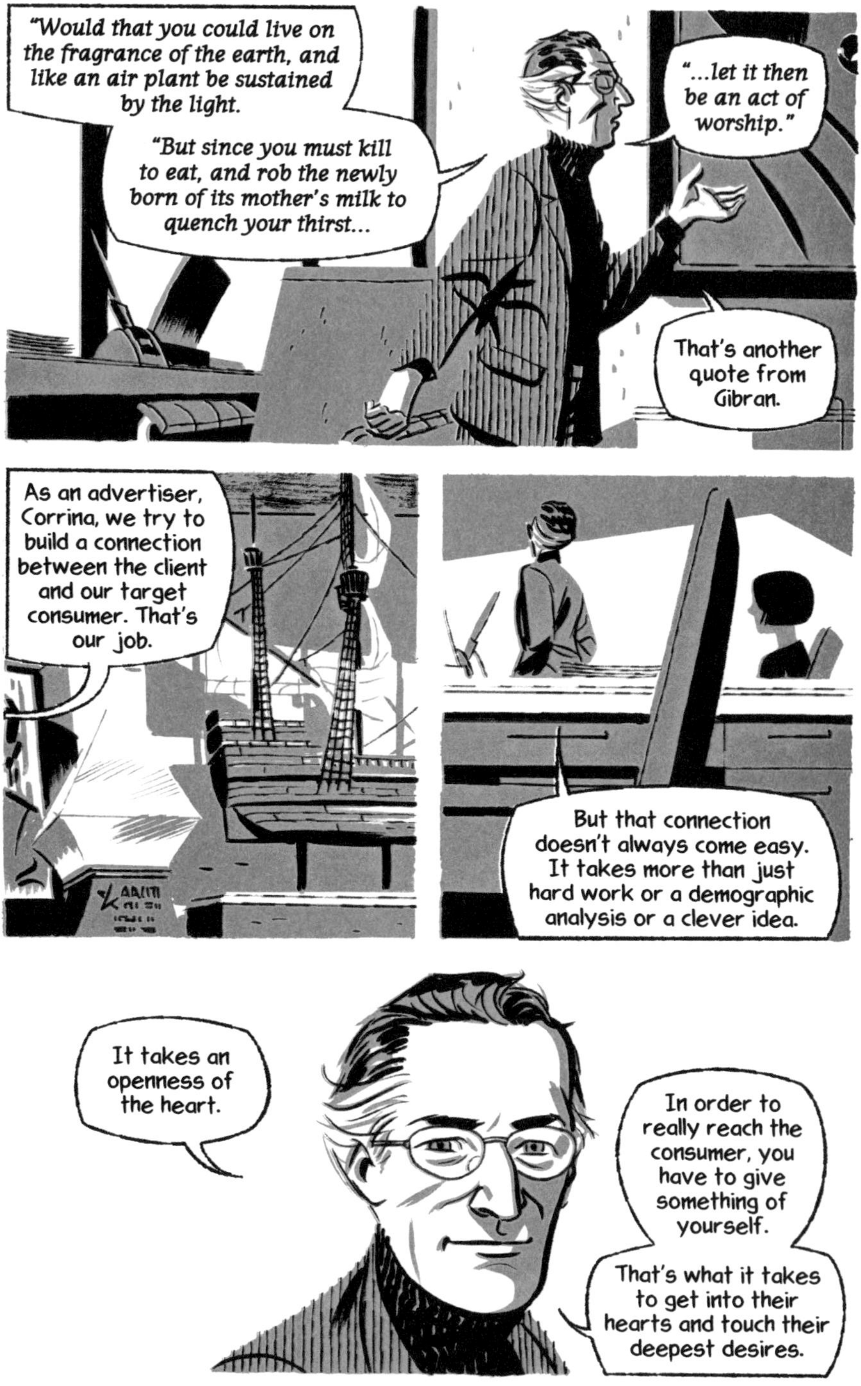
"Would that you could live on the fragrance of the earth, and like an air plant be sustained by the light.
"But since you must kill to eat, and rob the newly born of its mother's milk to quench your thirst...
"...let it then be an act of worship."
That's another quote from Gibran.
As an advertiser, Corrina, we try to build a connection between the client and our target consumer. That's our job.
But that connection doesn't always come easy. It takes more than just hard work or a demographic analysis or a clever idea.
It takes an openness of the heart.
In order to really reach the consumer, you have to give something of yourself.
That's what it takes to get into their hearts and touch their deepest desires.

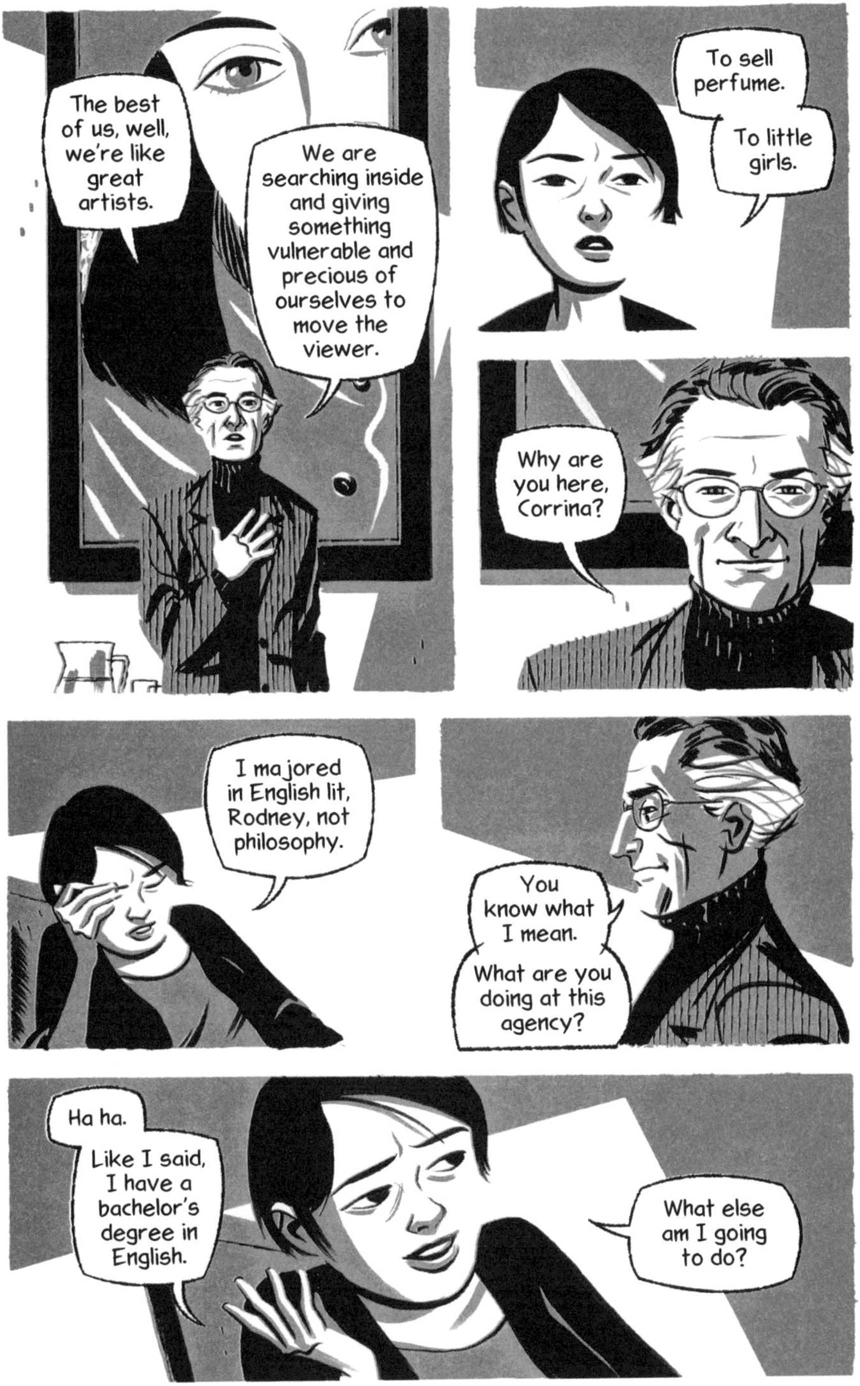

The best of us, well, we're like great artists.
We are searching inside and giving something vulnerable and precious of ourselves to move the viewer.
To sell perfume.
To little girls.
Why are you here, Corrina?
I majored in English lit, Rodney, not philosophy.
You know what I mean.
What are you doing at this agency?
Ha ha.
Like I said, I have a bachelor's degree in English.
What else am I going to do?

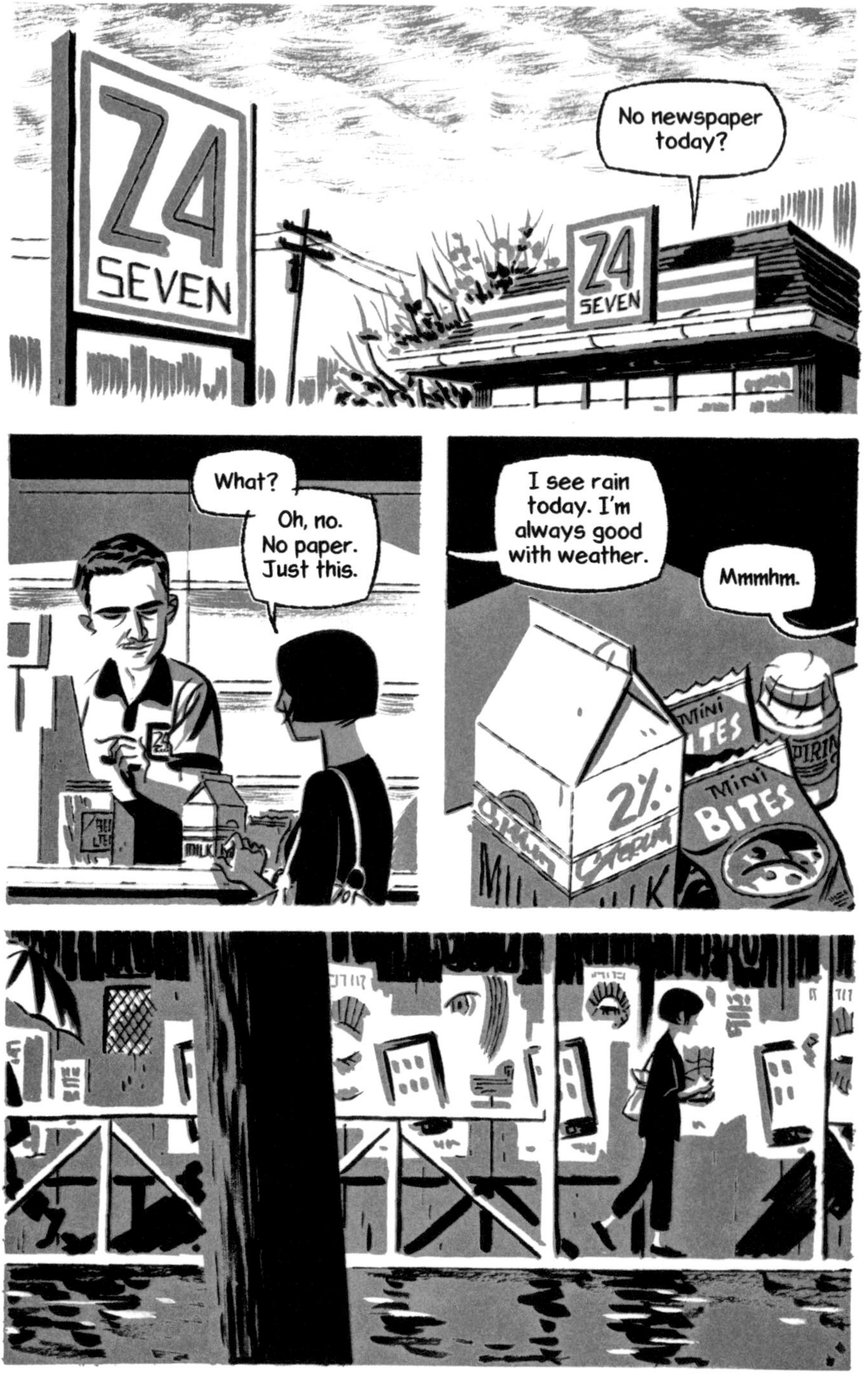
24 SEVEN
24 SEVEN
No newspaper today?
What?
Oh, no. No paper. Just this.
I see rain today. I'm always good with weather.
Mmmhm.
2%
MINI BITES

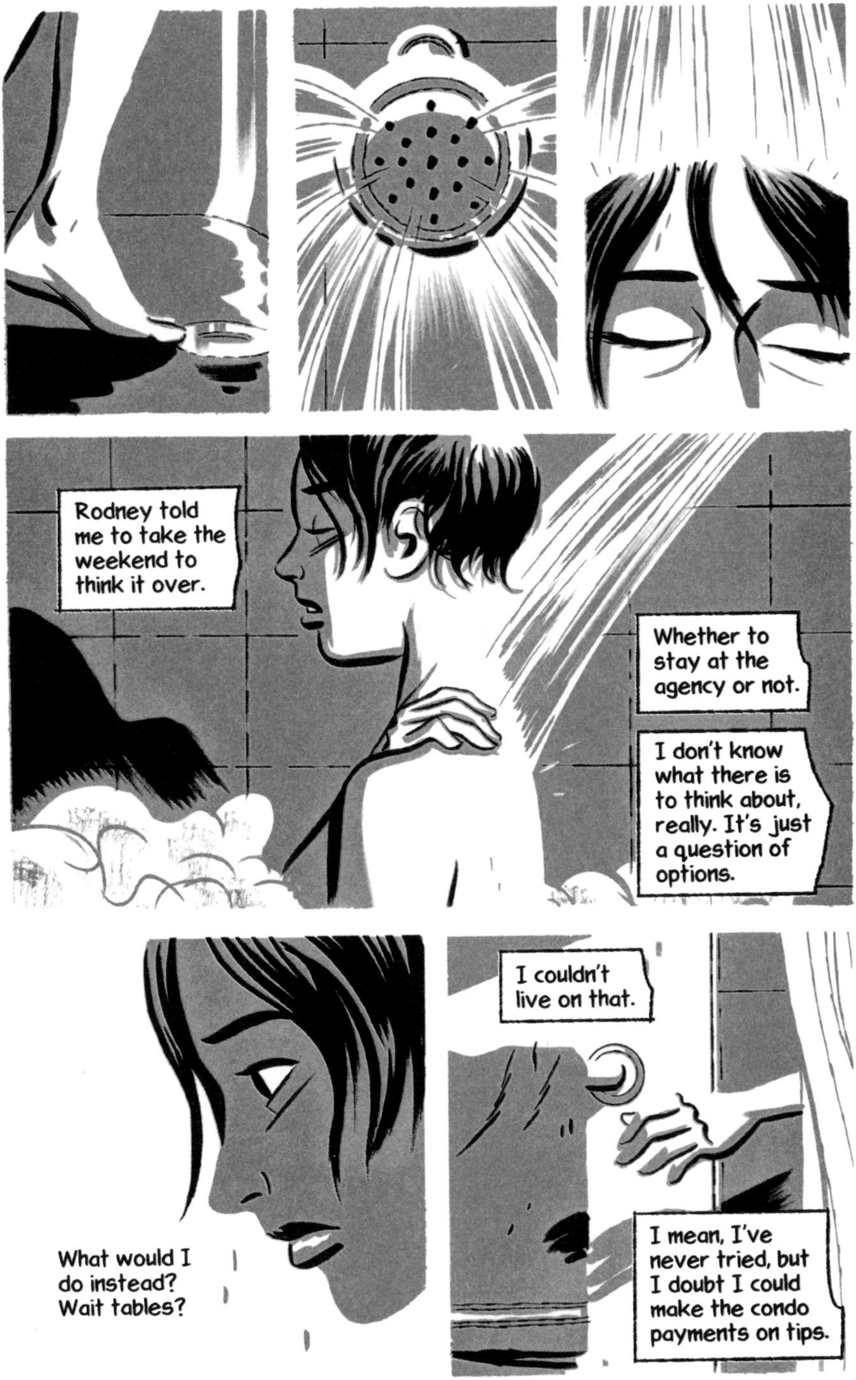
Rodney told me to take the weekend to think it over.
Whether to stay at the agency or not.
I don't know what there is to think about, really. It's just a question of options.
What would I do instead? Wait tables?
I couldn't live on that.
I mean, I've never tried, but I doubt I could make the condo payments on tips.

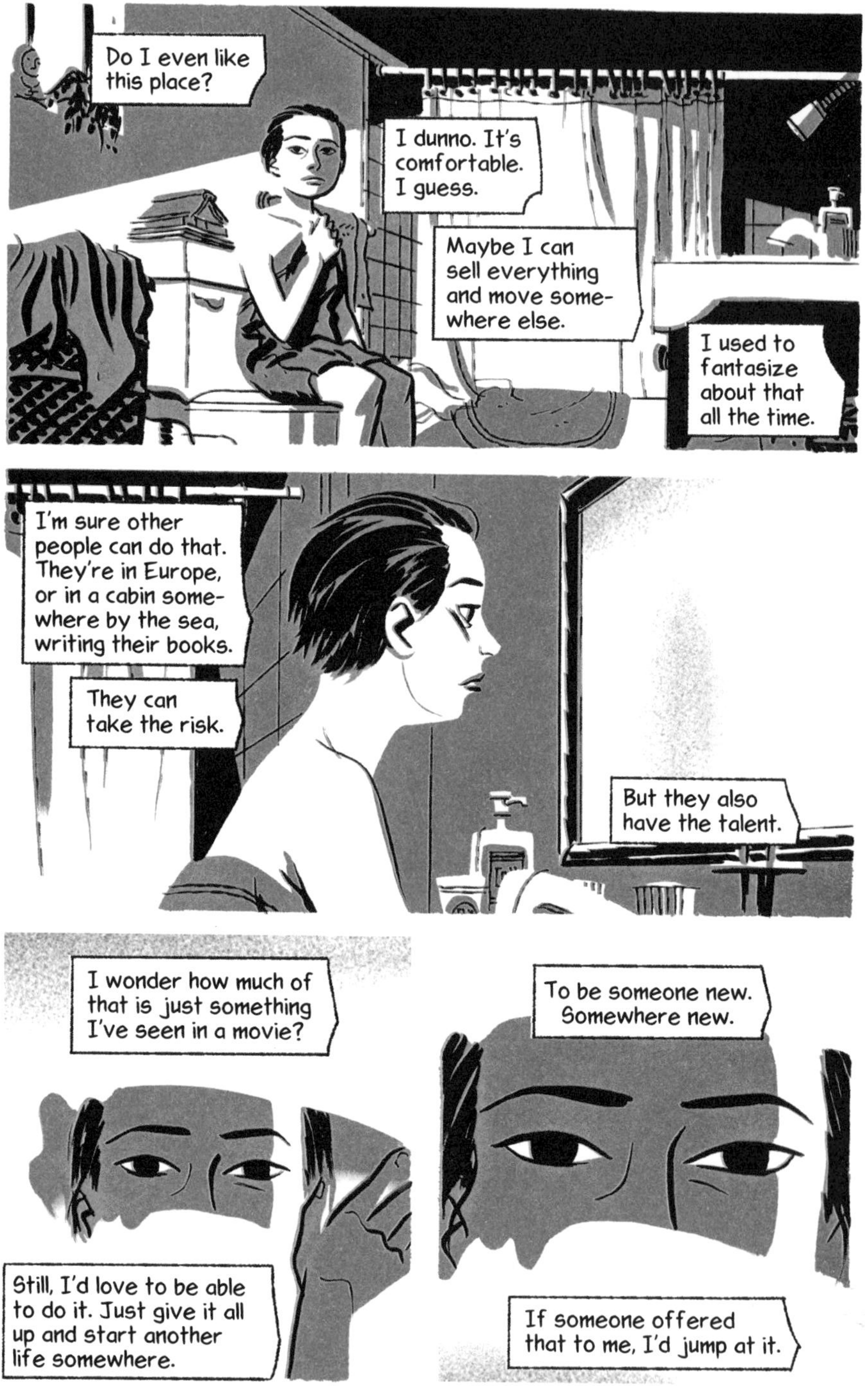
Do I even like this place?
I dunno. It's comfortable. I guess.
Maybe I can sell everything and move some-where else.
I used to fantasize about that all the time.
I'm sure other people can do that. They're in Europe, or in a cabin some-where by the sea, writing their books.
They can take the risk.
But they also have the talent.
I wonder how much of that is just something I've seen in a movie?
Still, I'd love to be able to do it. Just give it all up and start another life somewhere.
To be someone new. Somewhere new.
If someone offered that to me, I'd jump at it.

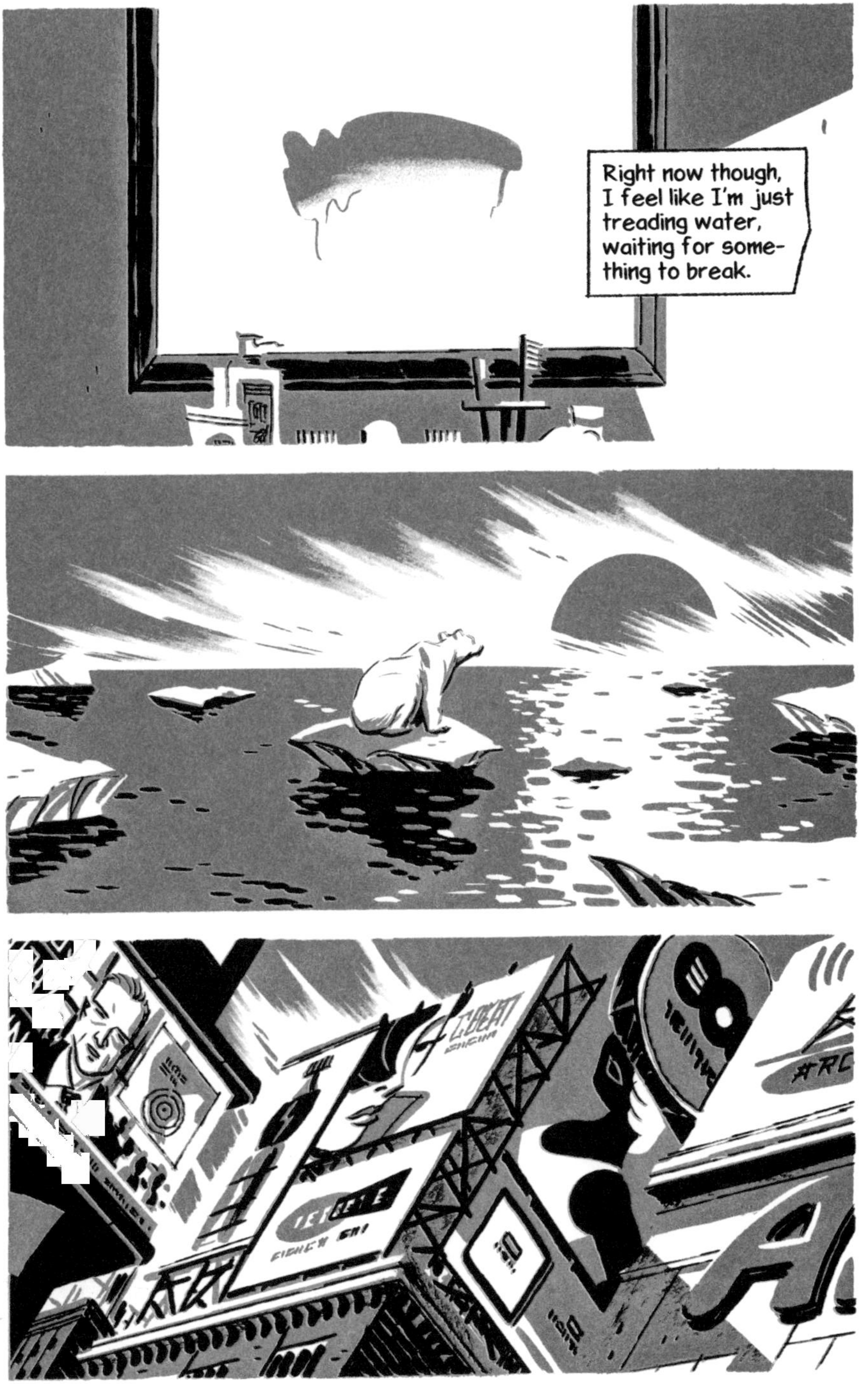
Right now though, I feel like I'm just treading water, waiting for something to break.

GRRRRR

You can complain all you want. It's the same food as yesterday. You ate it then.

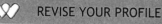

### REVISE YOUR PROFILE

*Our new editor makes sprucing up that profile a breeze!*

*Add emoticons now for only 2 tokens.*

**I spend a lot of time thinking about:**

*Traveling and seeing the world.*

**5 things I can't live without:**

1.
2.
3.
4.
5.

HSSSS!

sigh.

How about I eat with you, ok? Will that help?

Ugh.

RRING!

RRRING!

RRRING!

Hello?

Mraow?

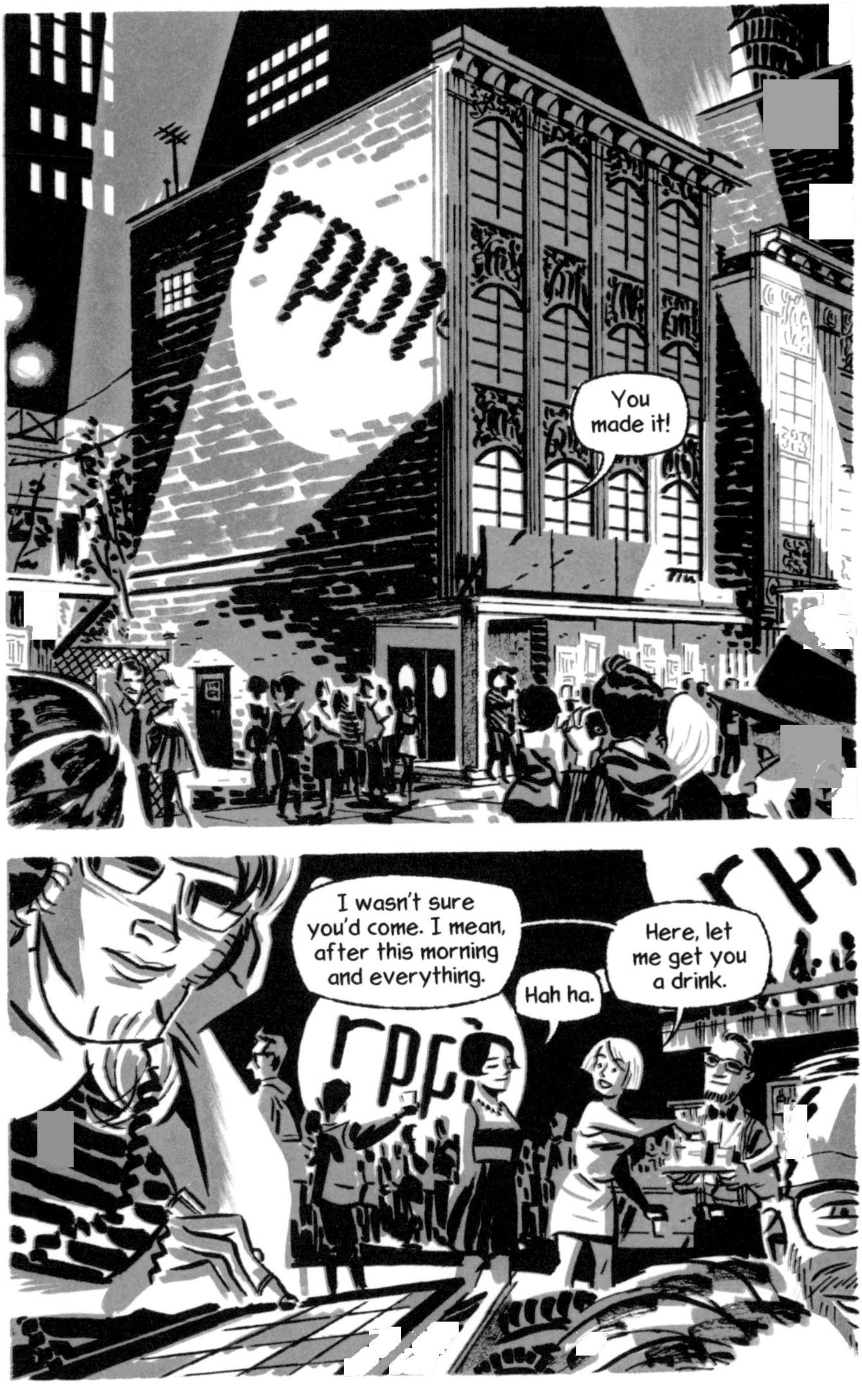
You made it!
I wasn't sure you'd come. I mean, after this morning and everything.
Hah ha.
Here, let me get you a drink.

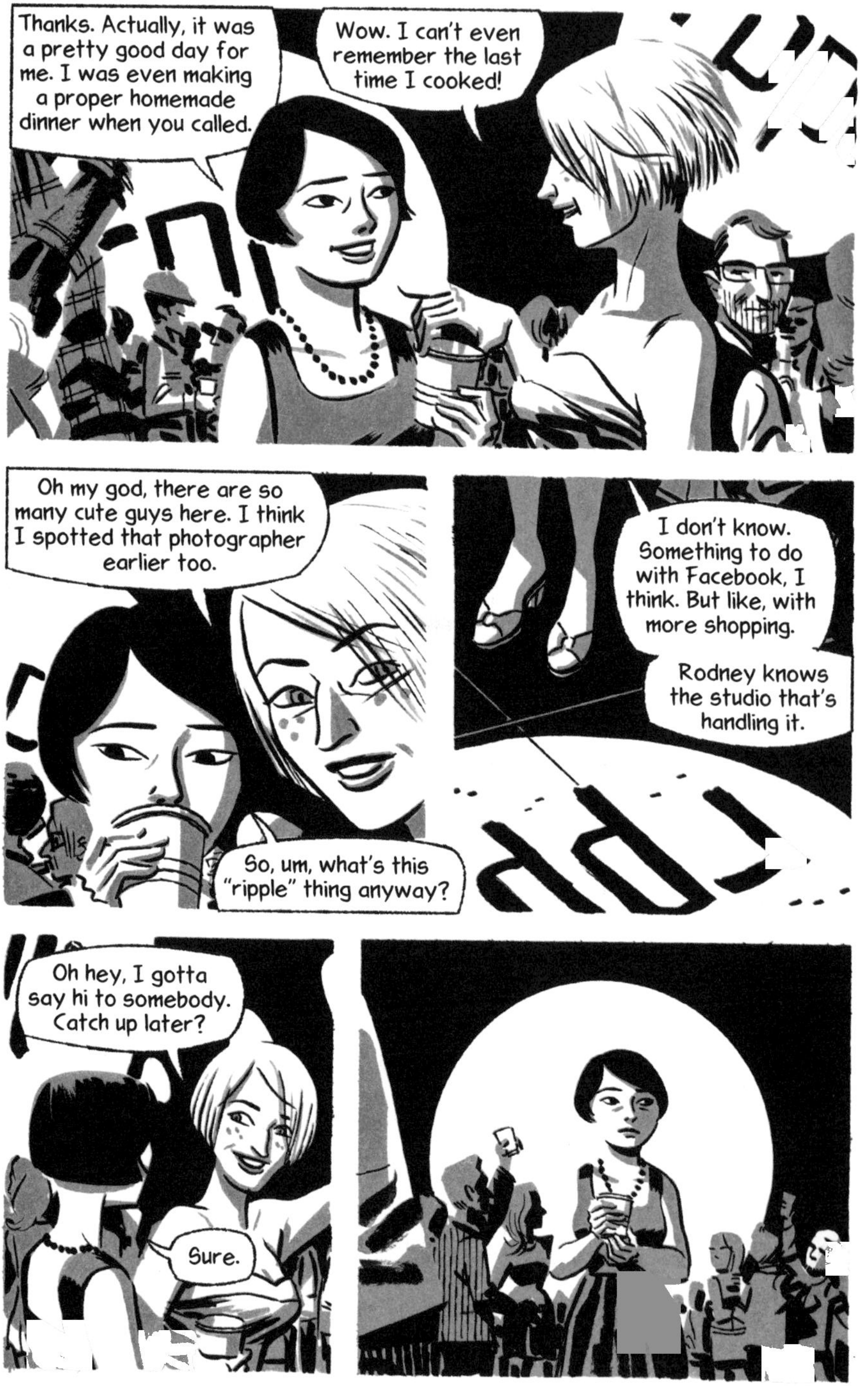
Thanks. Actually, it was a pretty good day for me. I was even making a proper homemade dinner when you called.
Wow. I can't even remember the last time I cooked!
Oh my god, there are so many cute guys here. I think I spotted that photographer earlier too.
So, um, what's this "ripple" thing anyway?
I don't know. Something to do with Facebook, I think. But like, with more shopping.
Rodney knows the studio that's handling it.
Oh hey, I gotta say hi to somebody. Catch up later?
Sure.

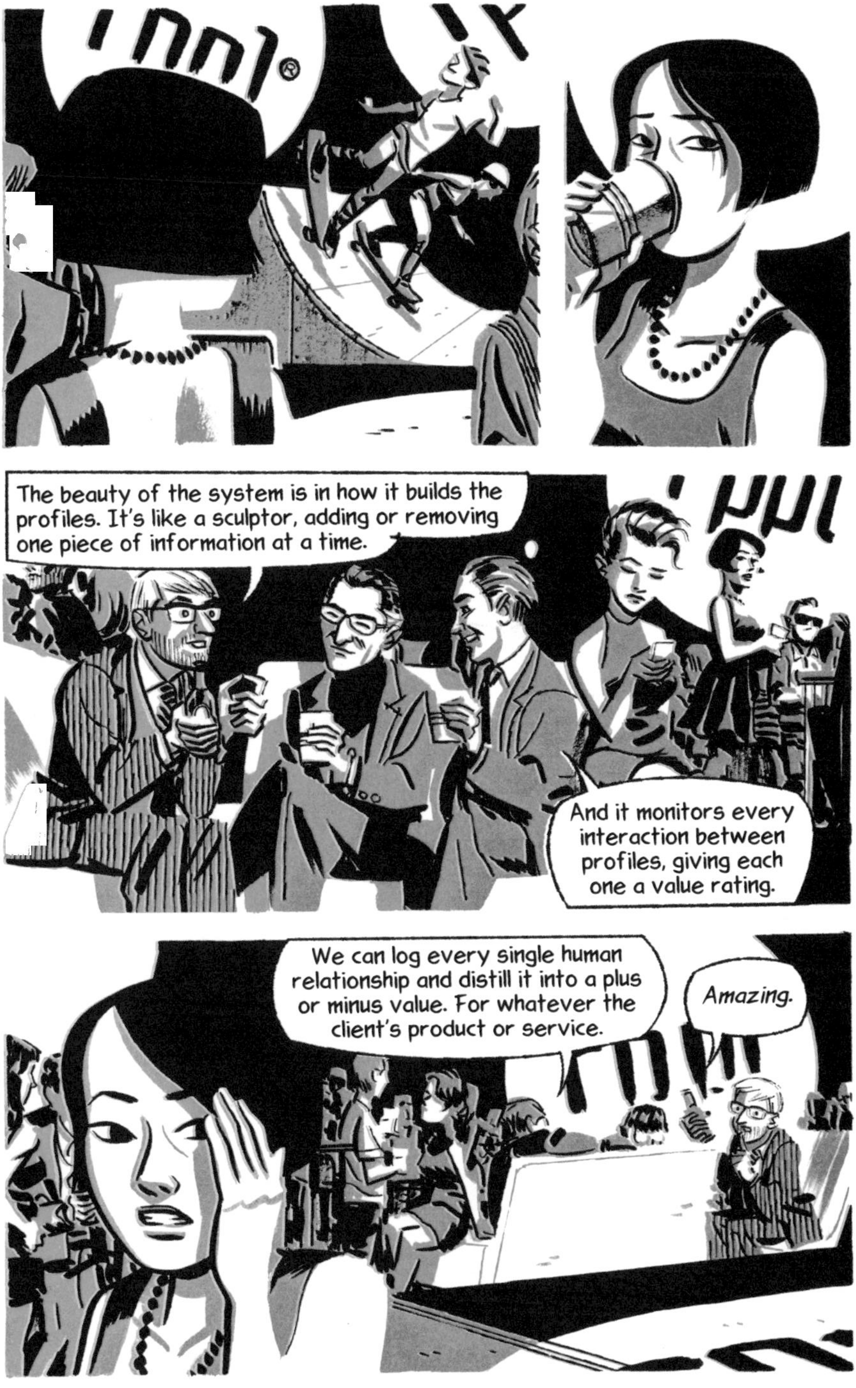
The beauty of the system is in how it builds the profiles. It's like a sculptor, adding or removing one piece of information at a time.
And it monitors every interaction between profiles, giving each one a value rating.
We can log every single human relationship and distill it into a plus or minus value. For whatever the client's product or service.
*Amazing.*

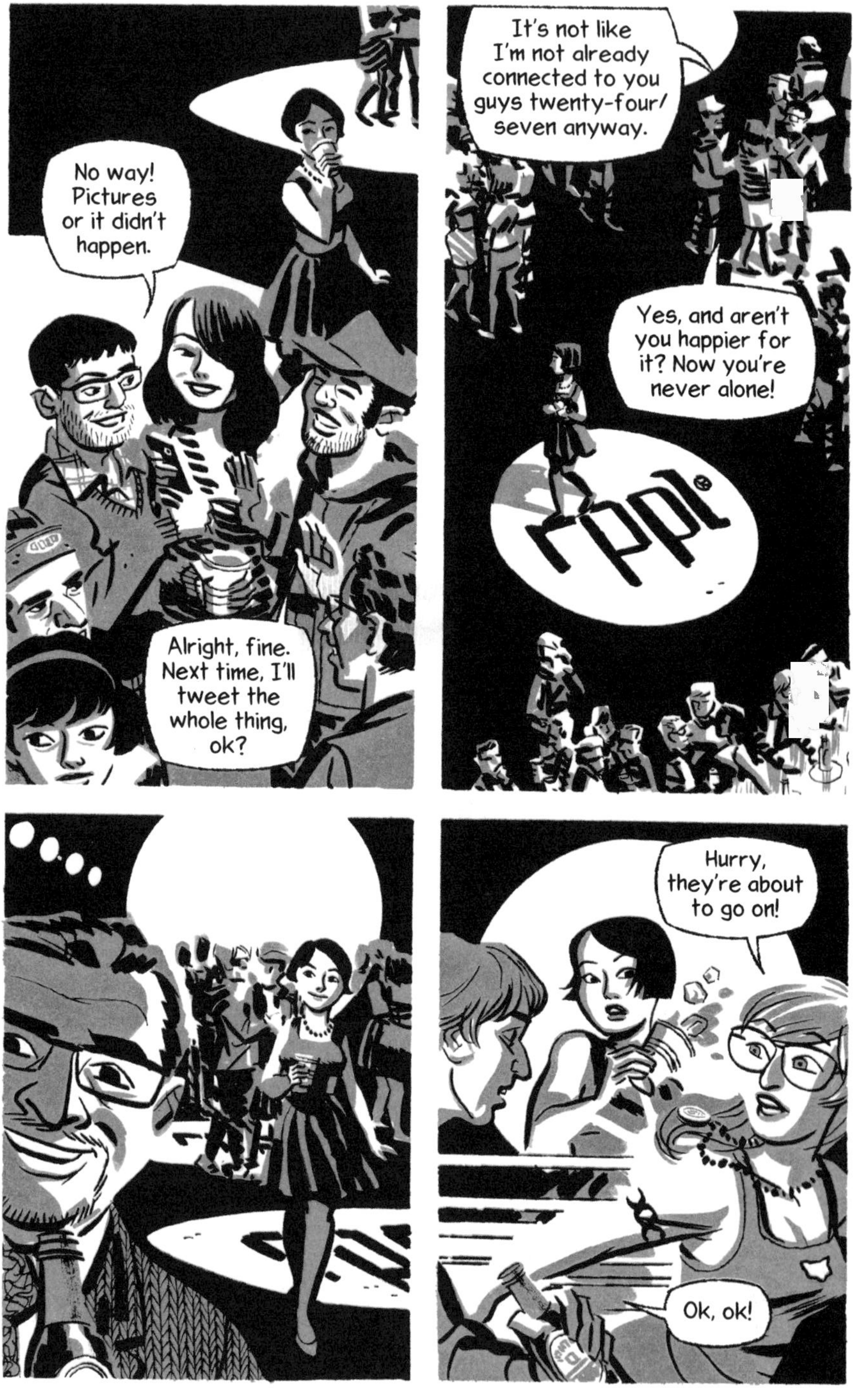
No way! Pictures or it didn't happen.
Alright, fine. Next time, I'll tweet the whole thing, ok?
It's not like I'm not already connected to you guys twenty-four/seven anyway.
Yes, and aren't you happier for it? Now you're never alone!
rppl
Hurry, they're about to go on!
Ok, ok!

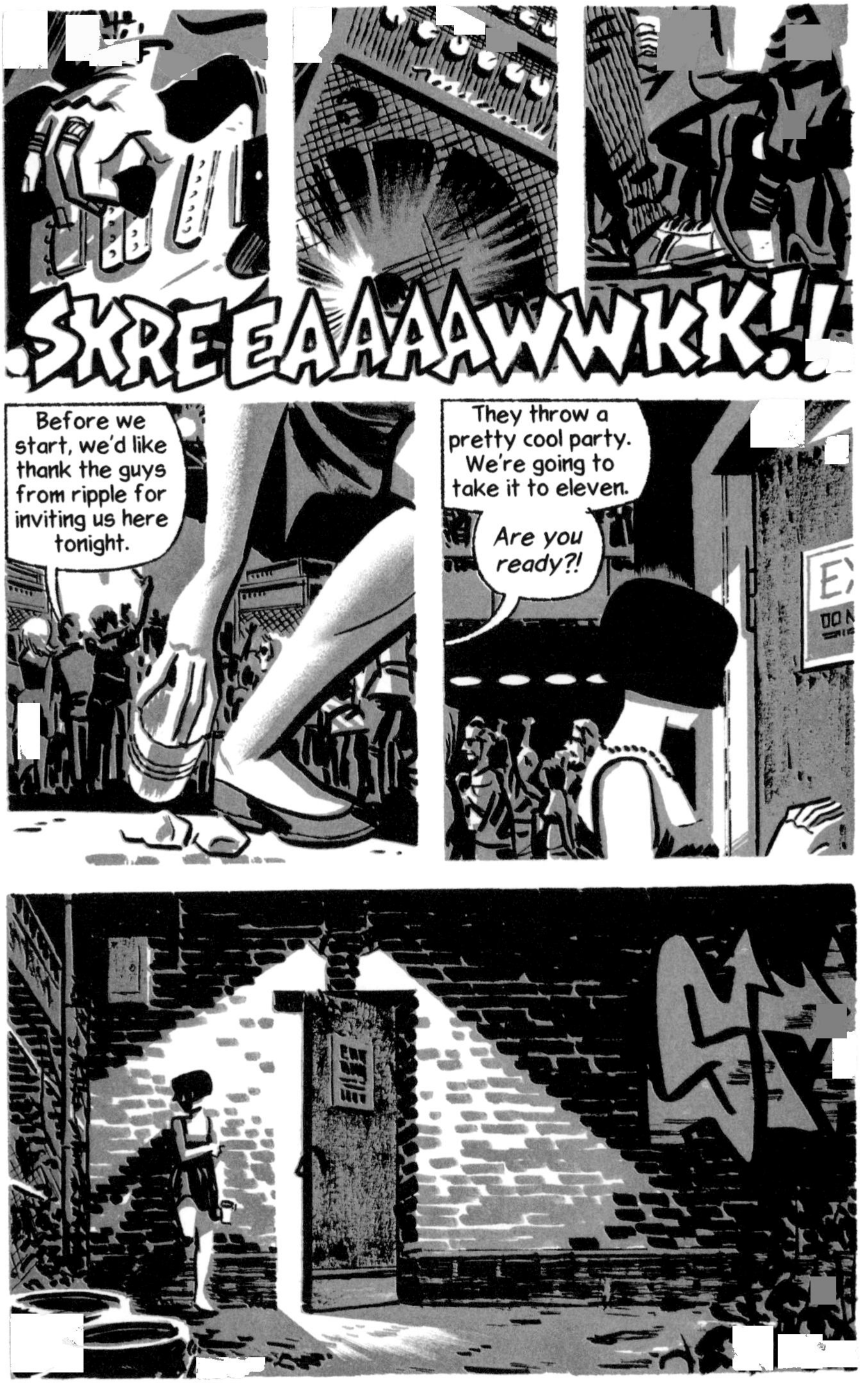
SKREEAAAAWWKK!!
Before we start, we'd like thank the guys from ripple for inviting us here tonight.
They throw a pretty cool party. We're going to take it to eleven.
Are you ready?!

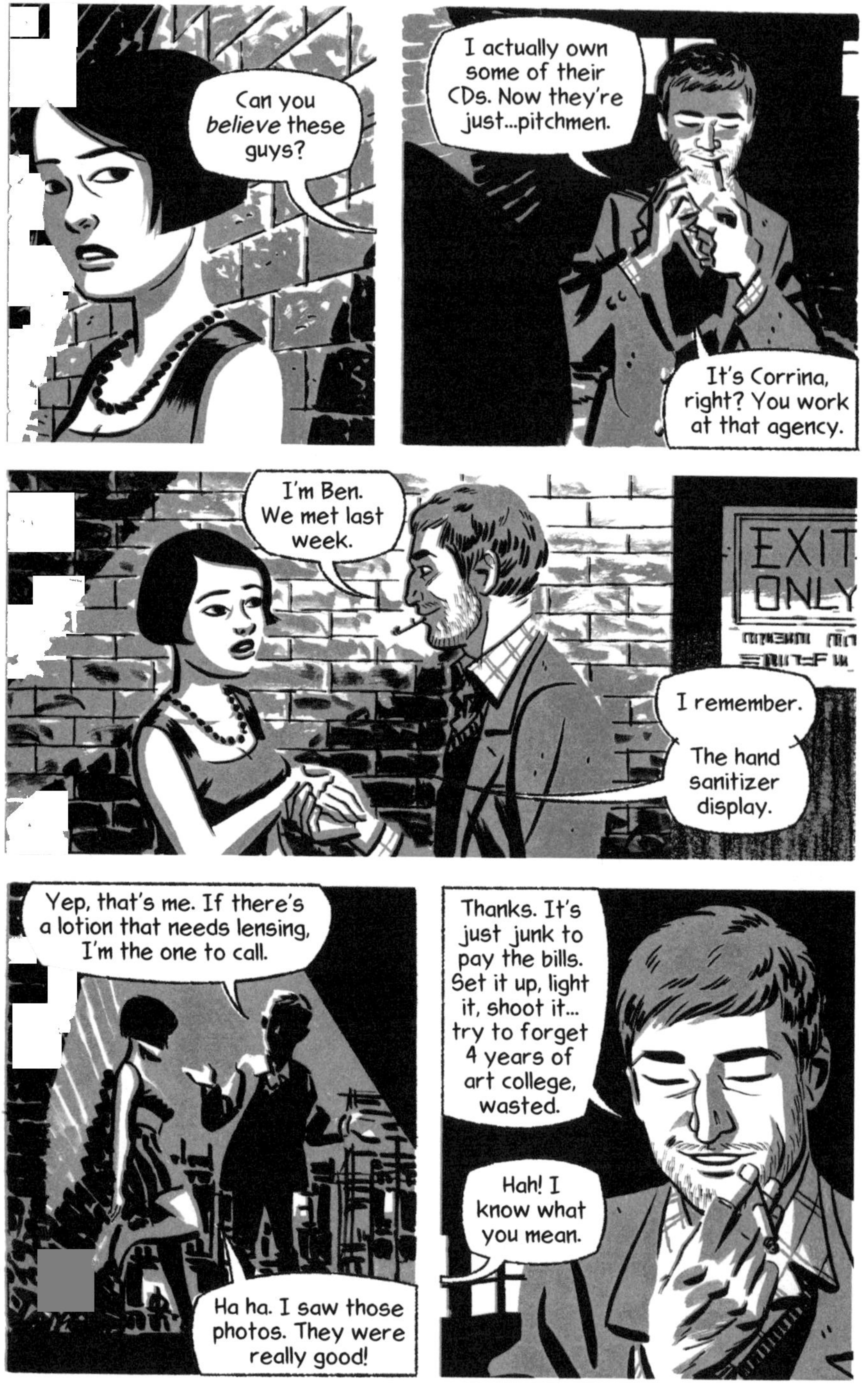
Can you *believe* these guys?
I actually own some of their CDs. Now they're just...pitchmen.
It's Corrina, right? You work at that agency.
I'm Ben. We met last week.
EXIT ONLY
I remember.
The hand sanitizer display.
Yep, that's me. If there's a lotion that needs lensing, I'm the one to call.
Ha ha. I saw those photos. They were really good!
Thanks. It's just junk to pay the bills. Set it up, light it, shoot it... try to forget 4 years of art college, wasted.
Hah! I know what you mean.

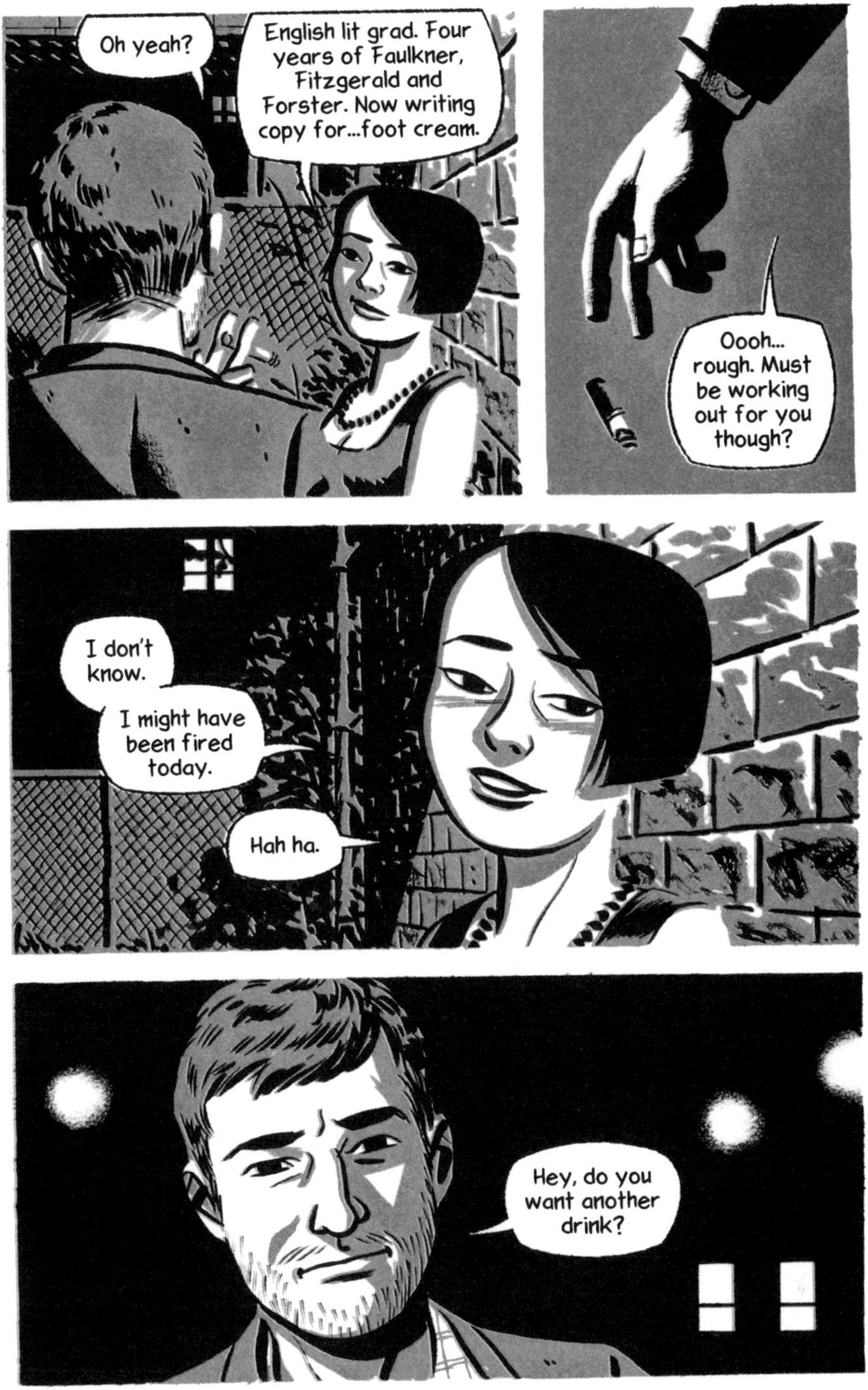
Oh yeah?
English lit grad. Four years of Faulkner, Fitzgerald and Forster. Now writing copy for...foot cream.
Oooh... rough. Must be working out for you though?
I don't know.
I might have been fired today.
Hah ha.
Hey, do you want another drink?

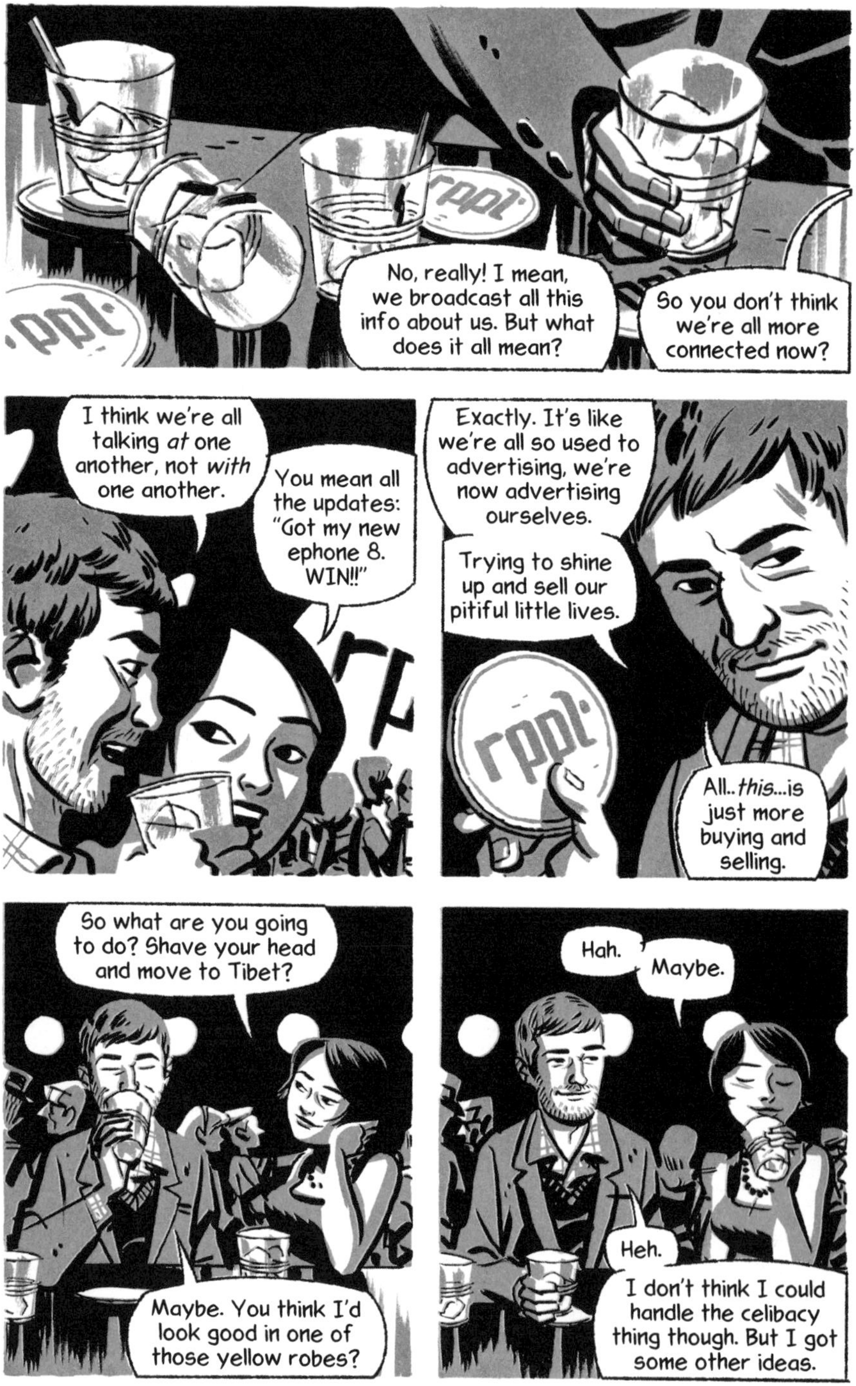

No, really! I mean, we broadcast all this info about us. But what does it all mean?
So you don't think we're all more connected now?
I think we're all talking *at* one another, not *with* one another.
You mean all the updates: "Got my new ephone 8. WIN!!"
Exactly. It's like we're all so used to advertising, we're now advertising ourselves.
Trying to shine up and sell our pitiful little lives.
All..*this*...is just more buying and selling.
So what are you going to do? Shave your head and move to Tibet?
Maybe. You think I'd look good in one of those yellow robes?
Hah.
Maybe.
Heh.
I don't think I could handle the celibacy thing though. But I got some other ideas.

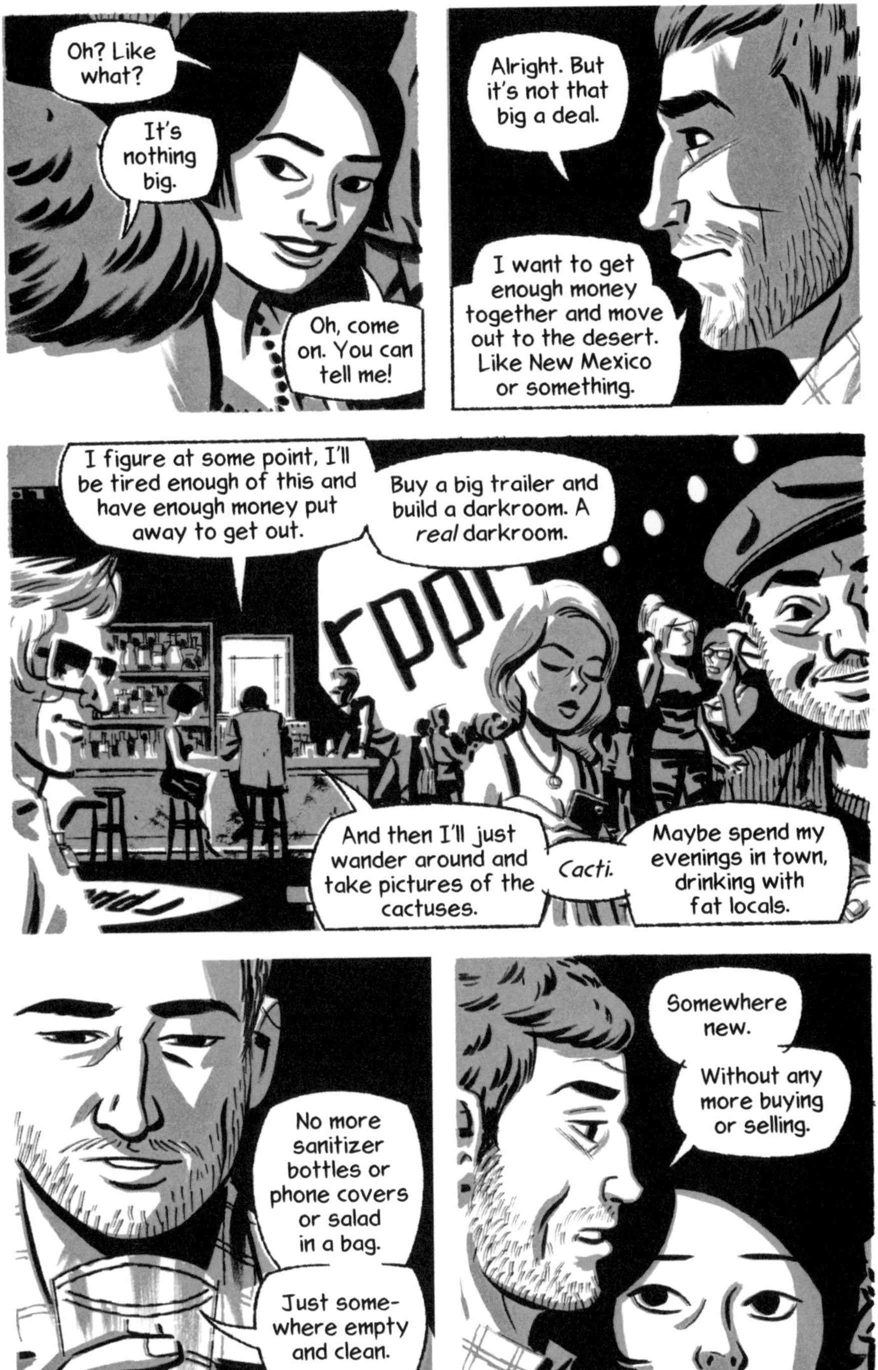
Oh? Like what?
It's nothing big.
Oh, come on. You can tell me!
Alright. But it's not that big a deal.
I want to get enough money together and move out to the desert. Like New Mexico or something.
I figure at some point, I'll be tired enough of this and have enough money put away to get out.
Buy a big trailer and build a darkroom. A *real* darkroom.
And then I'll just wander around and take pictures of the cactuses.
*Cacti.*
Maybe spend my evenings in town, drinking with fat locals.
No more sanitizer bottles or phone covers or salad in a bag.
Just some-where empty and clean.
Somewhere new.
Without any more buying or selling.

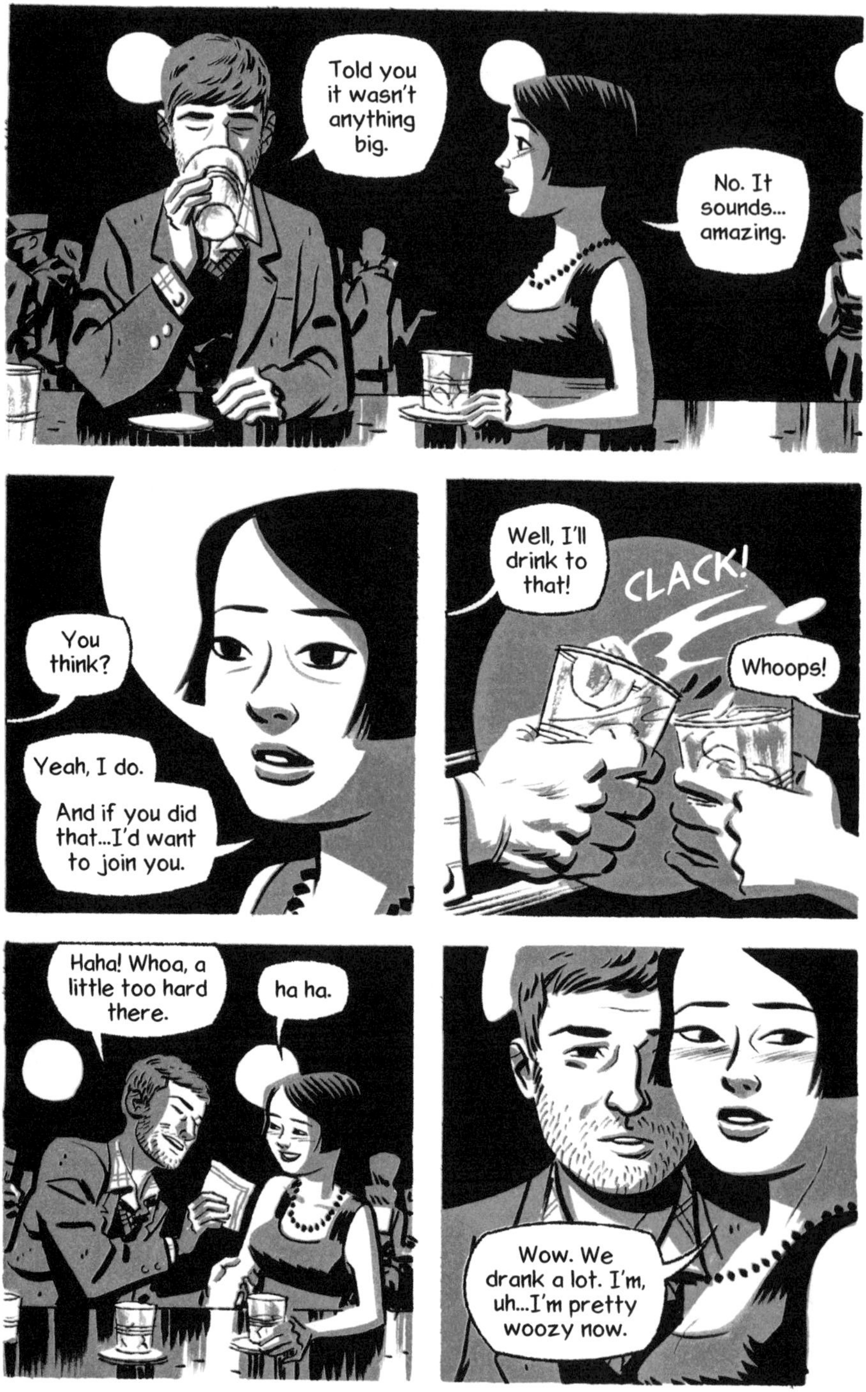
Told you it wasn't anything big.
No. It sounds... amazing.
You think?
Yeah, I do.
And if you did that...I'd want to join you.
Well, I'll drink to that!
CLACK!
Whoops!
Haha! Whoa, a little too hard there.
ha ha.
Wow. We drank a lot. I'm, uh...I'm pretty woozy now.

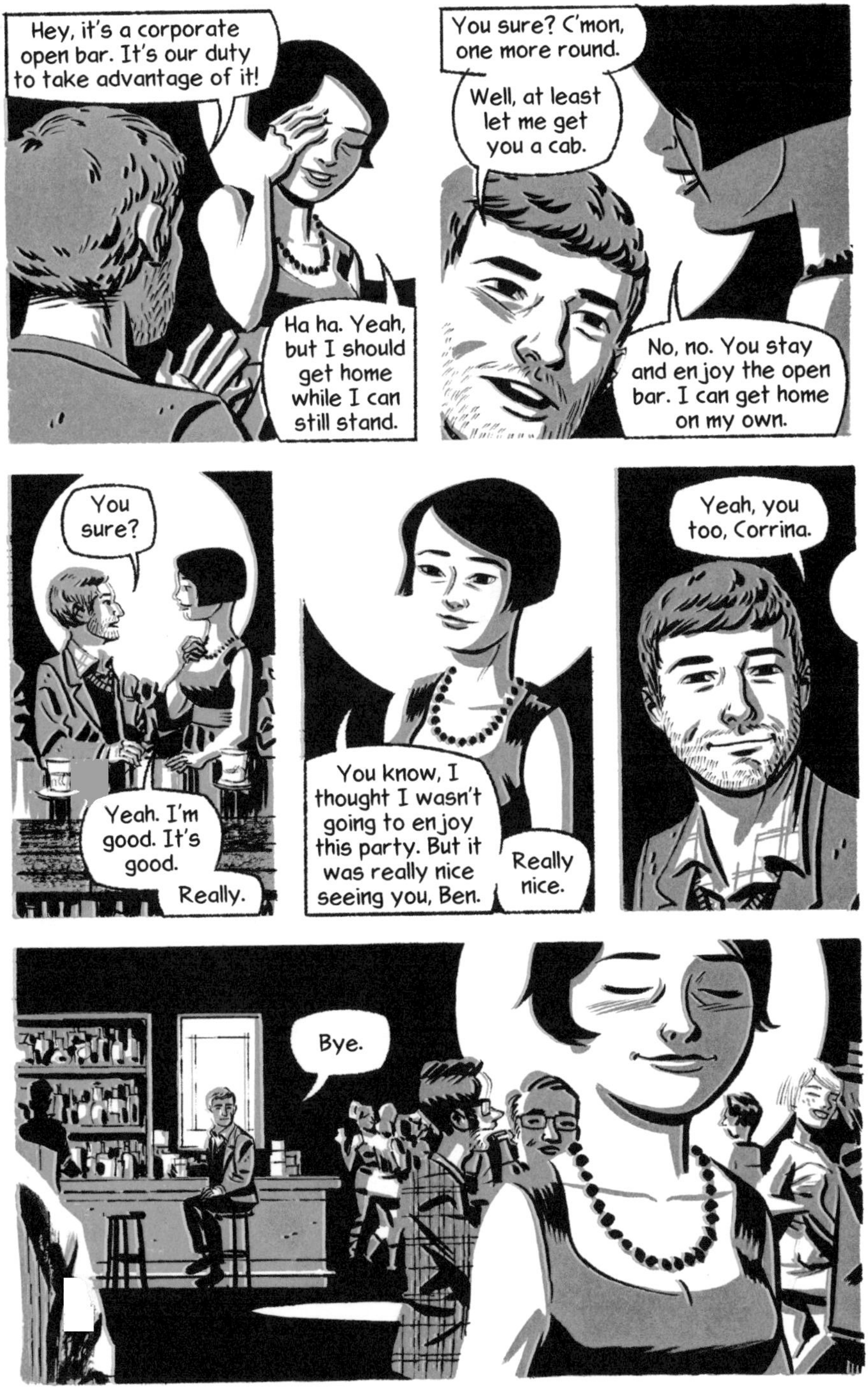
Hey, it's a corporate open bar. It's our duty to take advantage of it!
Ha ha. Yeah, but I should get home while I can still stand.
You sure? C'mon, one more round.
Well, at least let me get you a cab.
No, no. You stay and enjoy the open bar. I can get home on my own.
You sure?
Yeah. I'm good. It's good.
Really.
You know, I thought I wasn't going to enjoy this party. But it was really nice seeing you, Ben.
Really nice.
Yeah, you too, Corrina.
Bye.

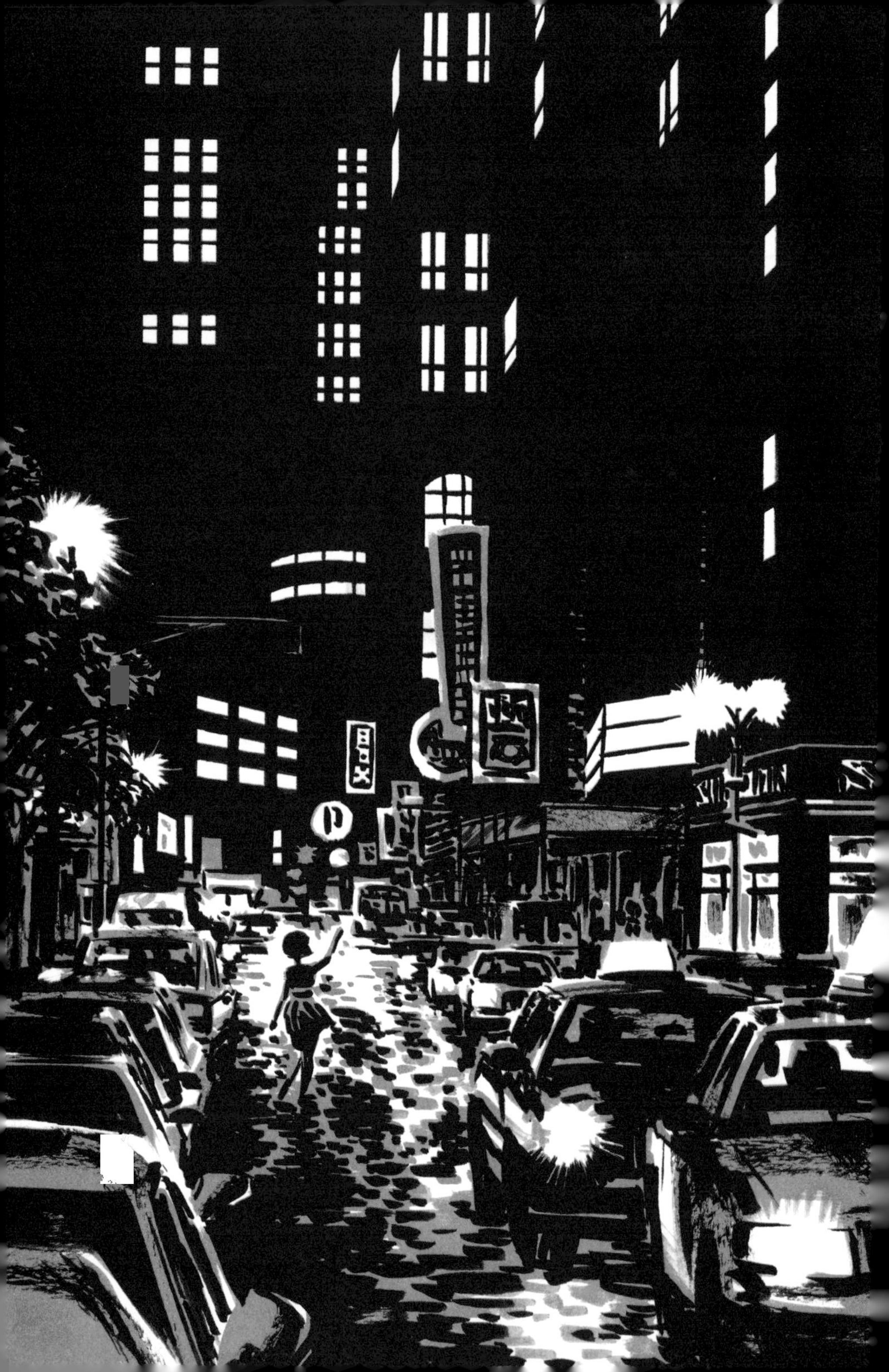

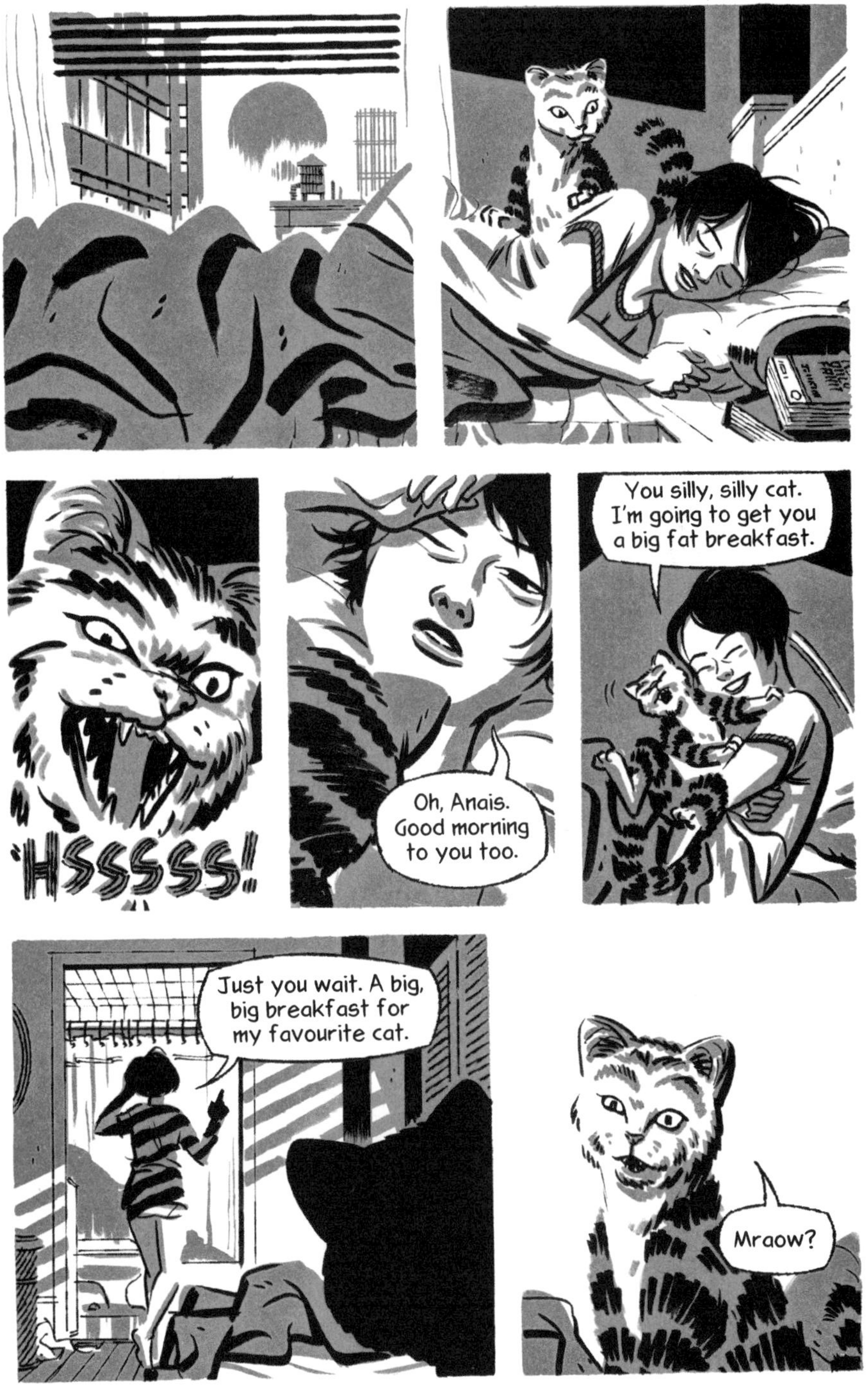
HSSSSS!
Oh, Anais. Good morning to you too.
You silly, silly cat. I'm going to get you a big fat breakfast.
Just you wait. A big, big breakfast for my favourite cat.
Mraow?

You know, sweetie, I should be way more hungover than I am.

I haven't gotten drunk like that in a long time.

God, I haven't had fun like that in, like... forever.

Ben Pine
PHOTOGRAPHY
(210) 5411-1711
benpinephoto@gmail.com

I knew I should have given him my number.

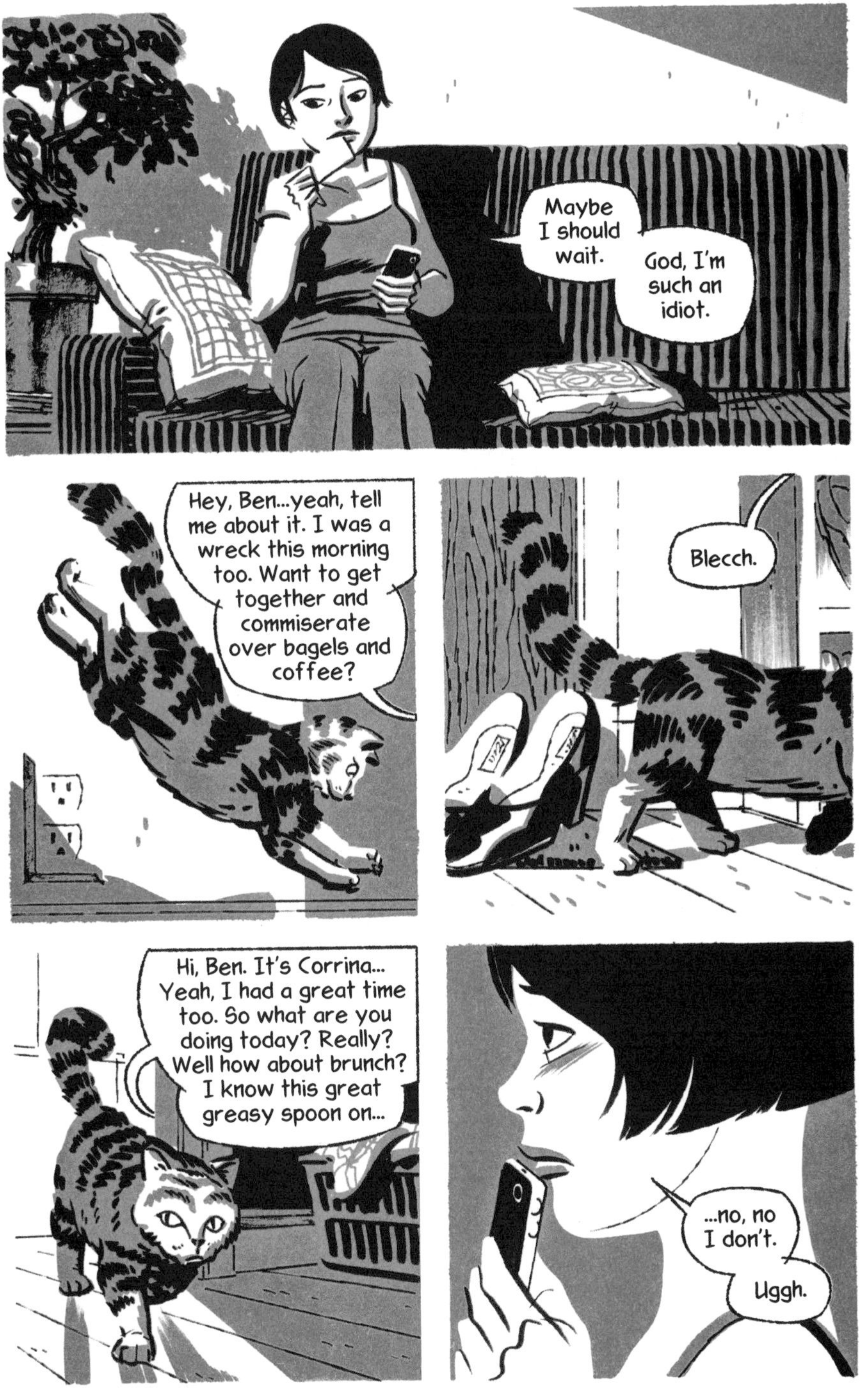

Maybe I should wait.
God, I'm such an idiot.
Hey, Ben...yeah, tell me about it. I was a wreck this morning too. Want to get together and commiserate over bagels and coffee?
Blecch.
Hi, Ben. It's Corrina... Yeah, I had a great time too. So what are you doing today? Really? Well how about brunch? I know this great greasy spoon on...
...no, no I don't.
Uggh.

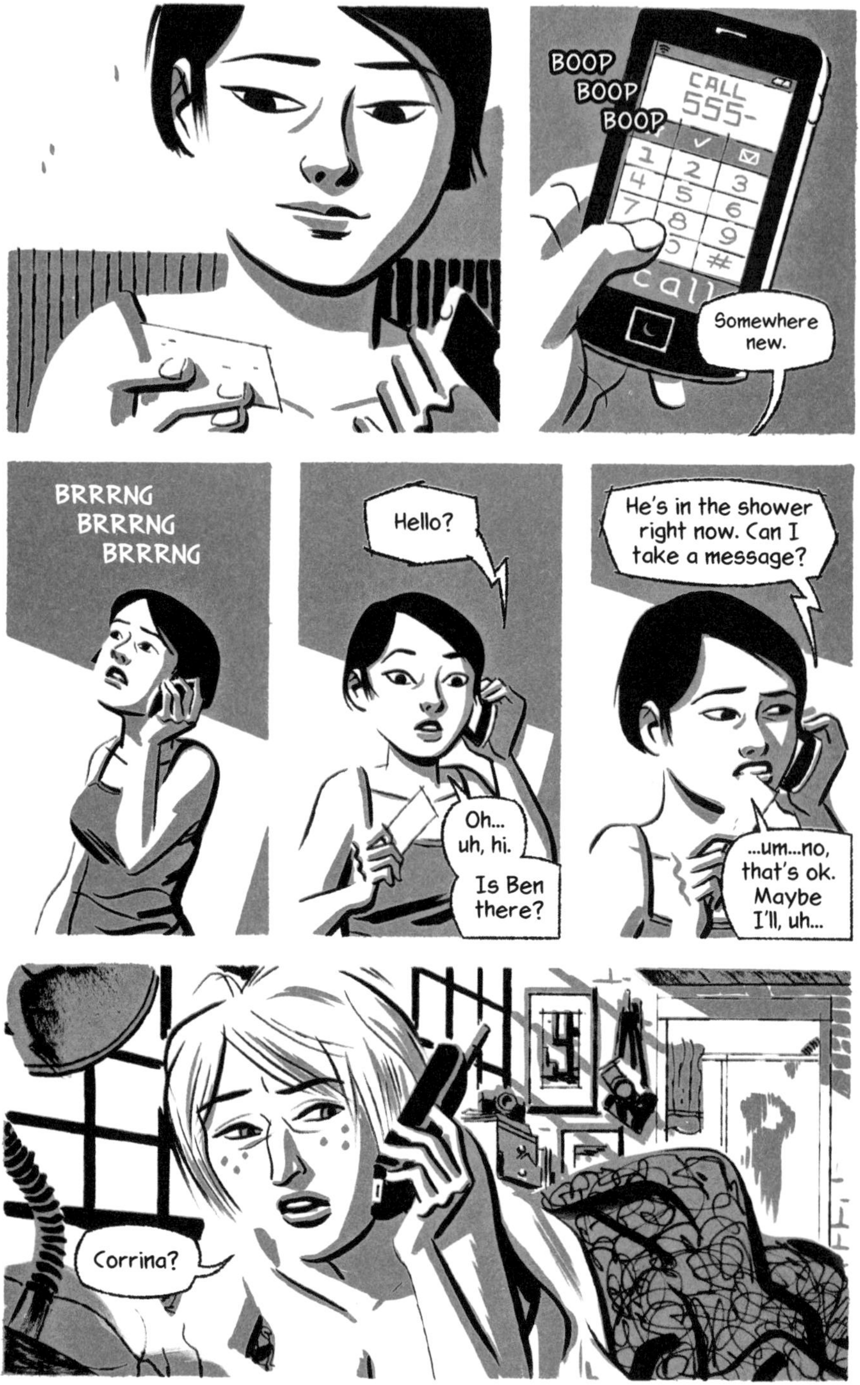
BOOP
BOOP
BOOP
CALL
555-
1
2
3
4
5
6
7
8
9
#
call
Somewhere new.
BRRRNG
BRRRNG
BRRRNG
Hello?
Oh... uh, hi.
Is Ben there?
He's in the shower right now. Can I take a message?
...um...no, that's ok. Maybe I'll, uh...
Corrina?

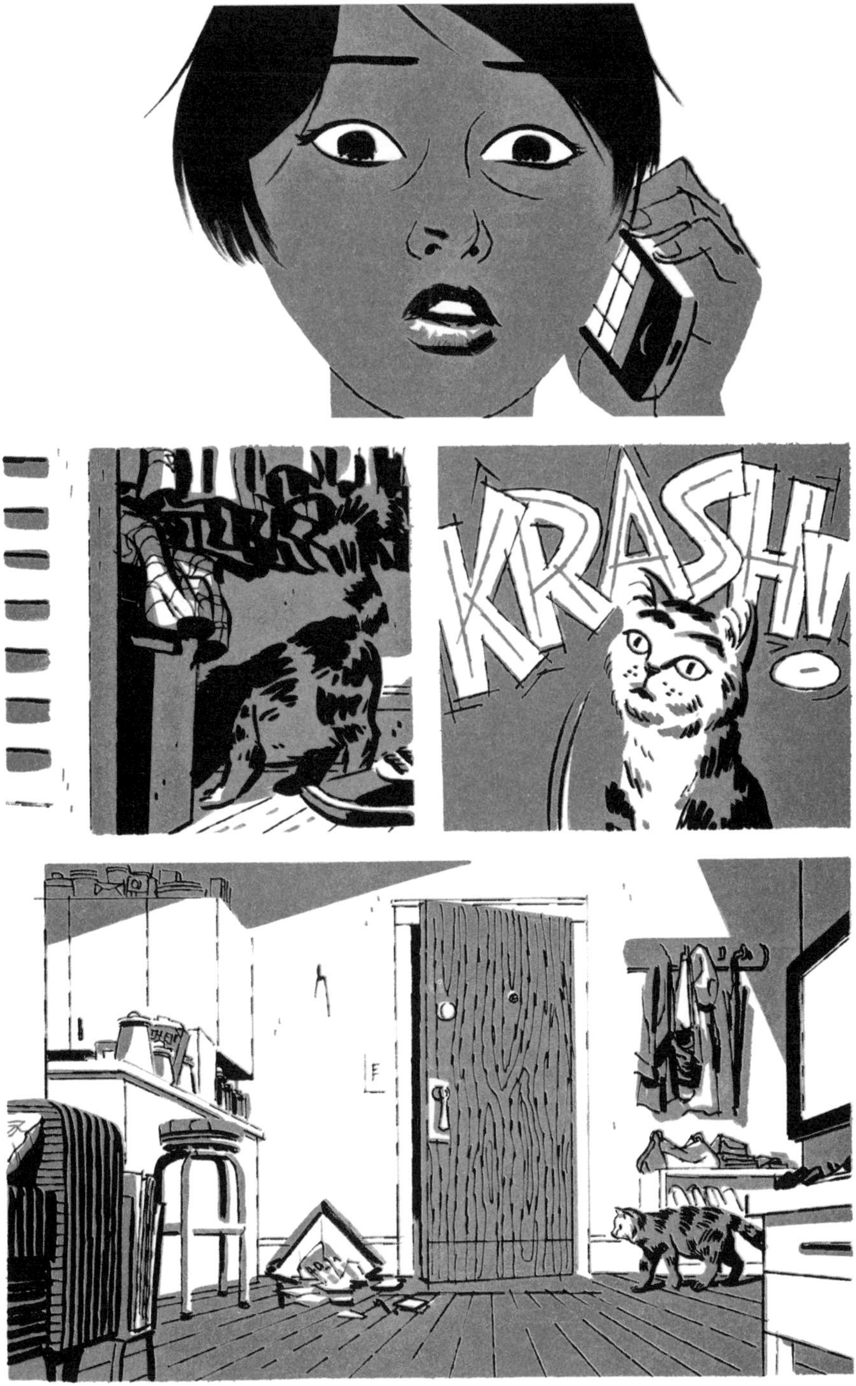
KRASH!

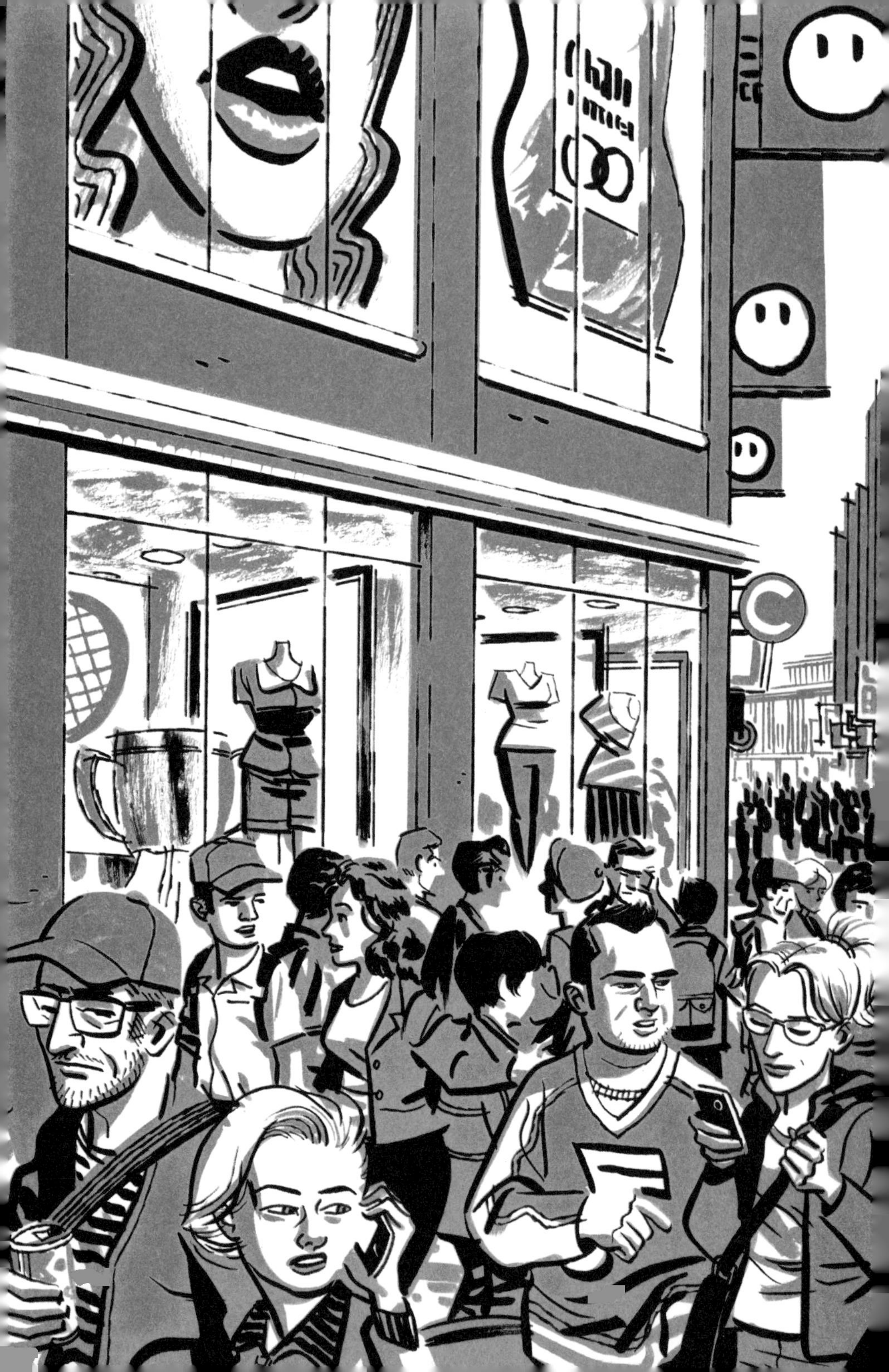

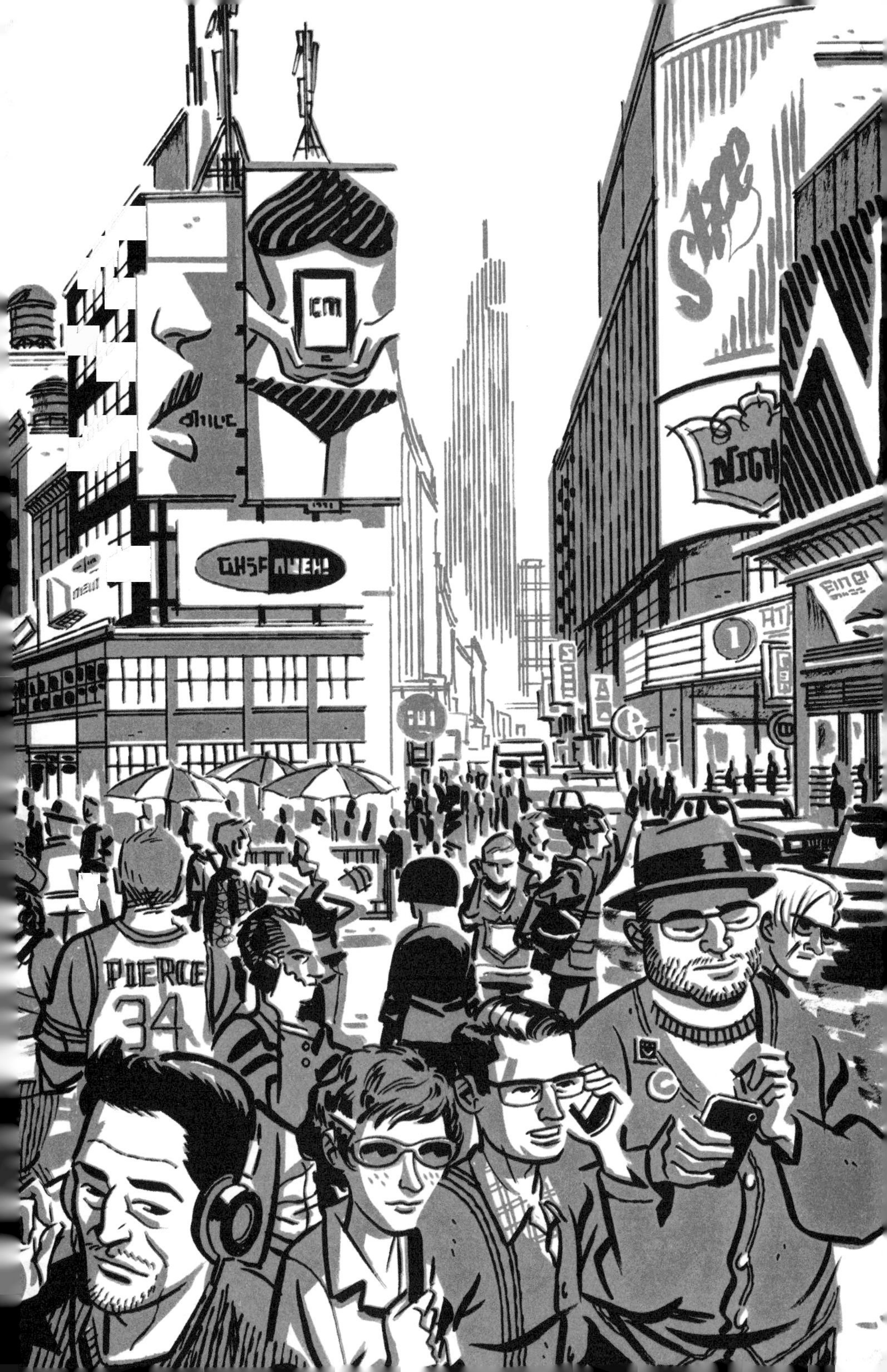
PIERCE
34

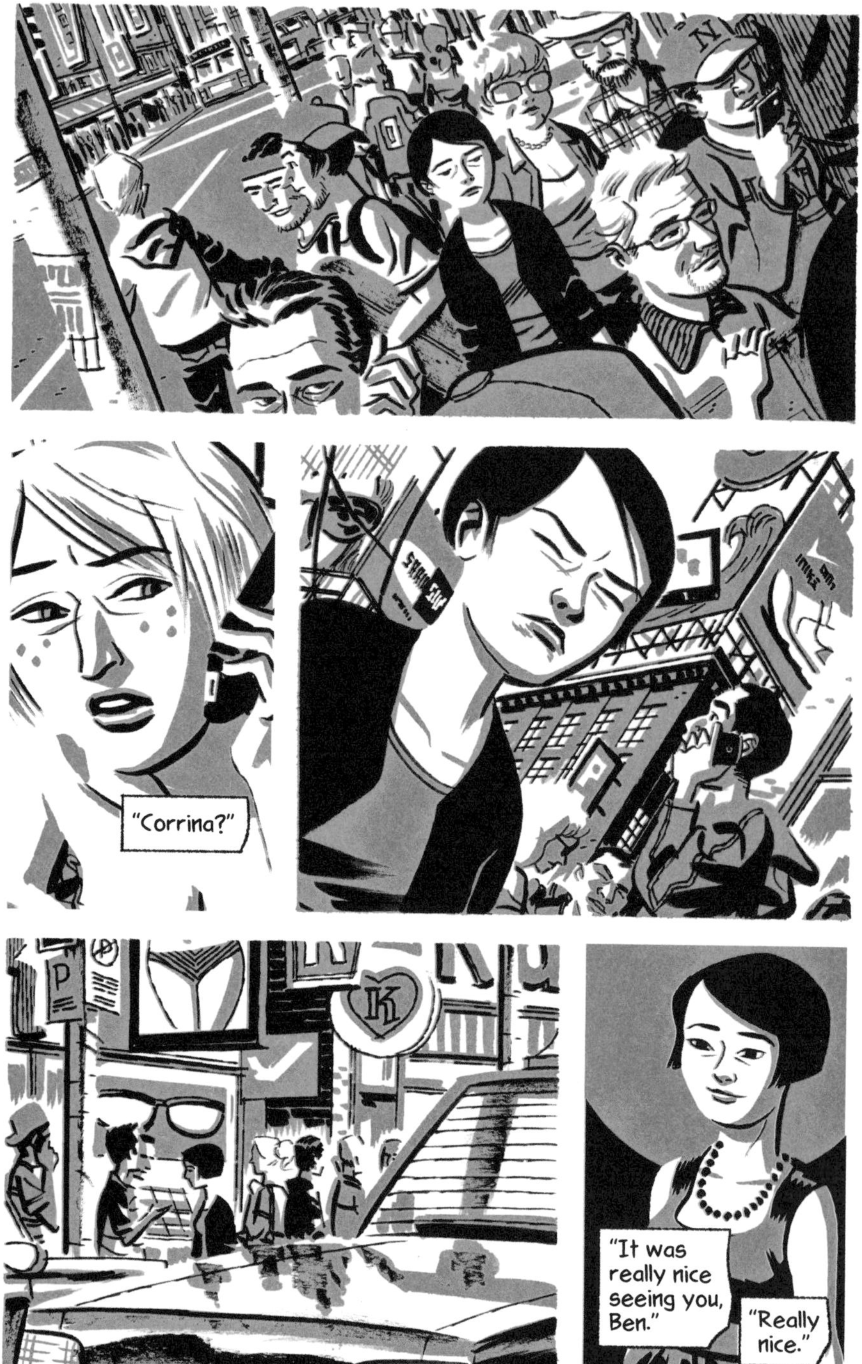
"Corrina?"
"It was really nice seeing you, Ben."
"Really nice."

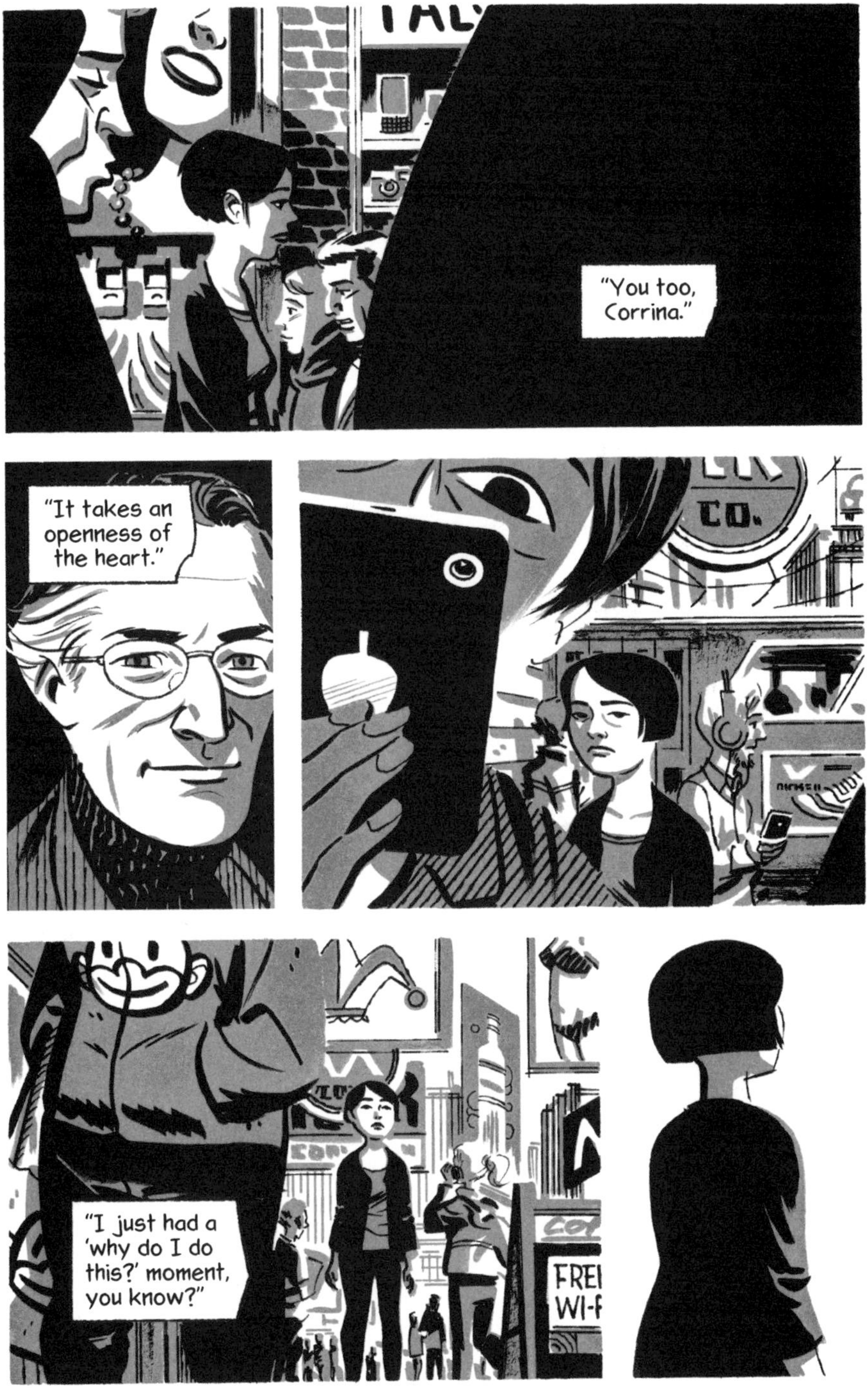
"You too, Corrina."
"It takes an openness of the heart."
"I just had a 'why do I do this?' moment, you know?"

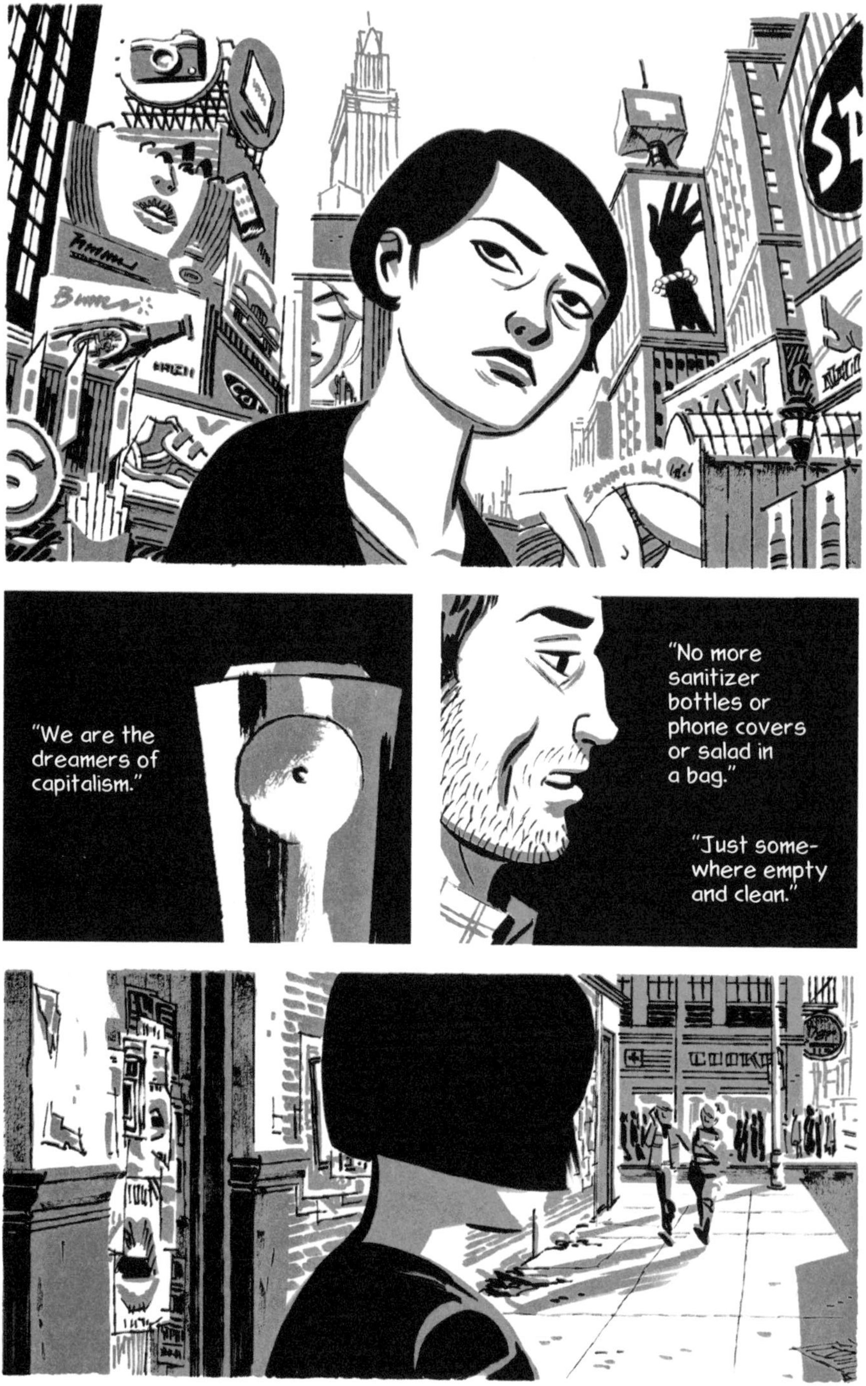
"We are the dreamers of capitalism."
"No more sanitizer bottles or phone covers or salad in a bag."
"Just some-where empty and clean."

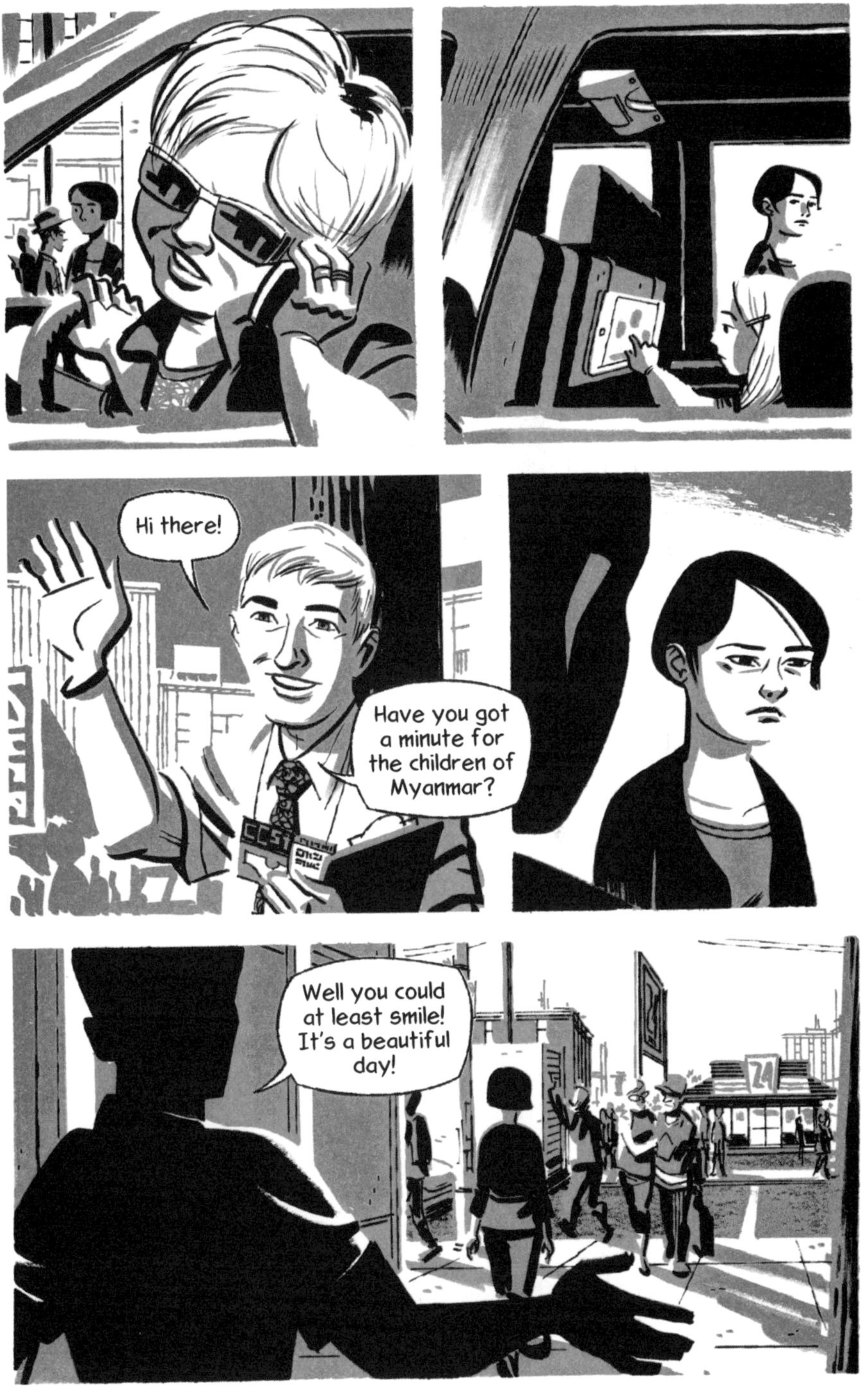
Hi there!
Have you got a minute for the children of Myanmar?
Well you could at least smile! It's a beautiful day!
24

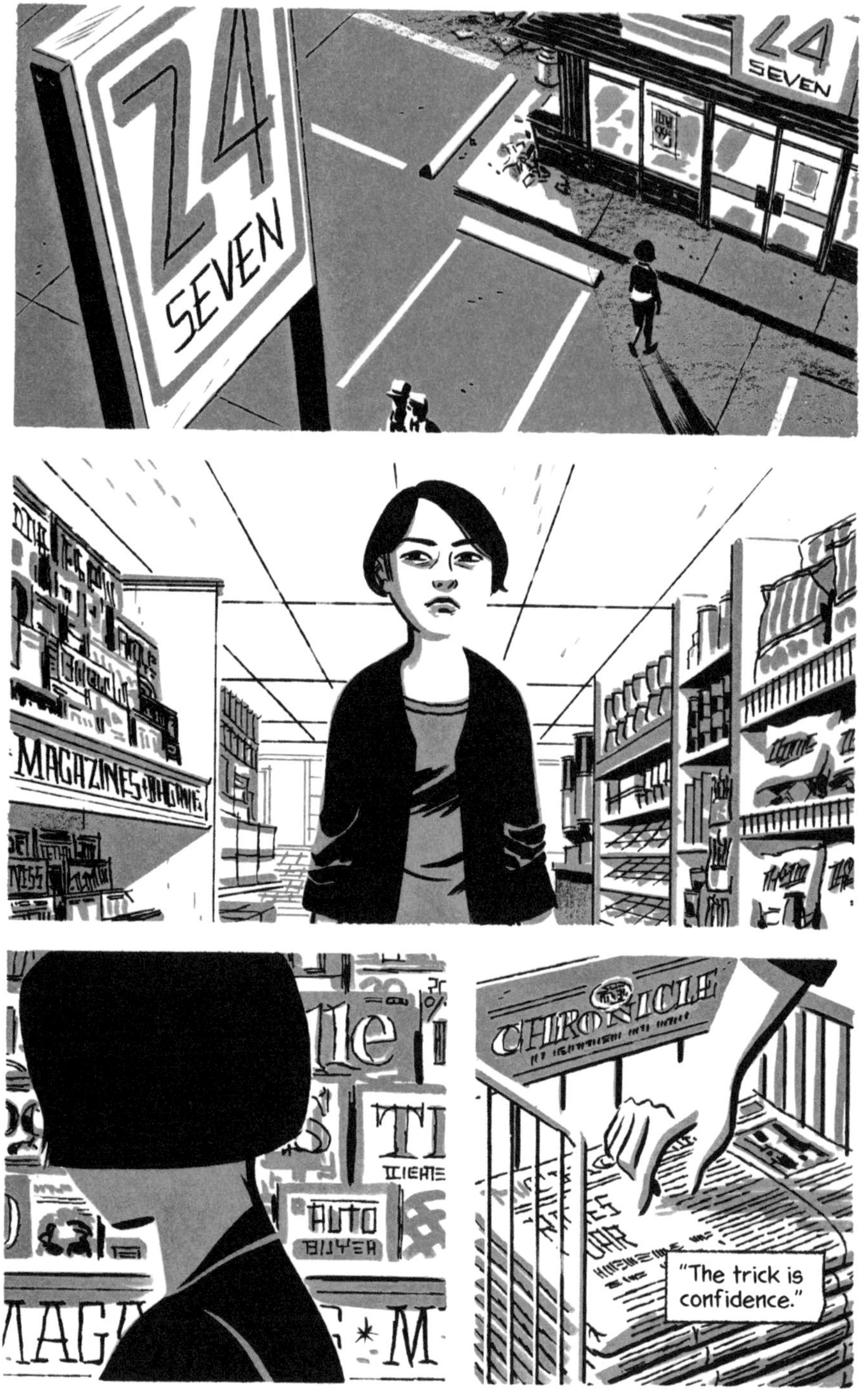
24 SEVEN
24 SEVEN
MAGAZINES
CHRONICLE
AUTO
"The trick is confidence."

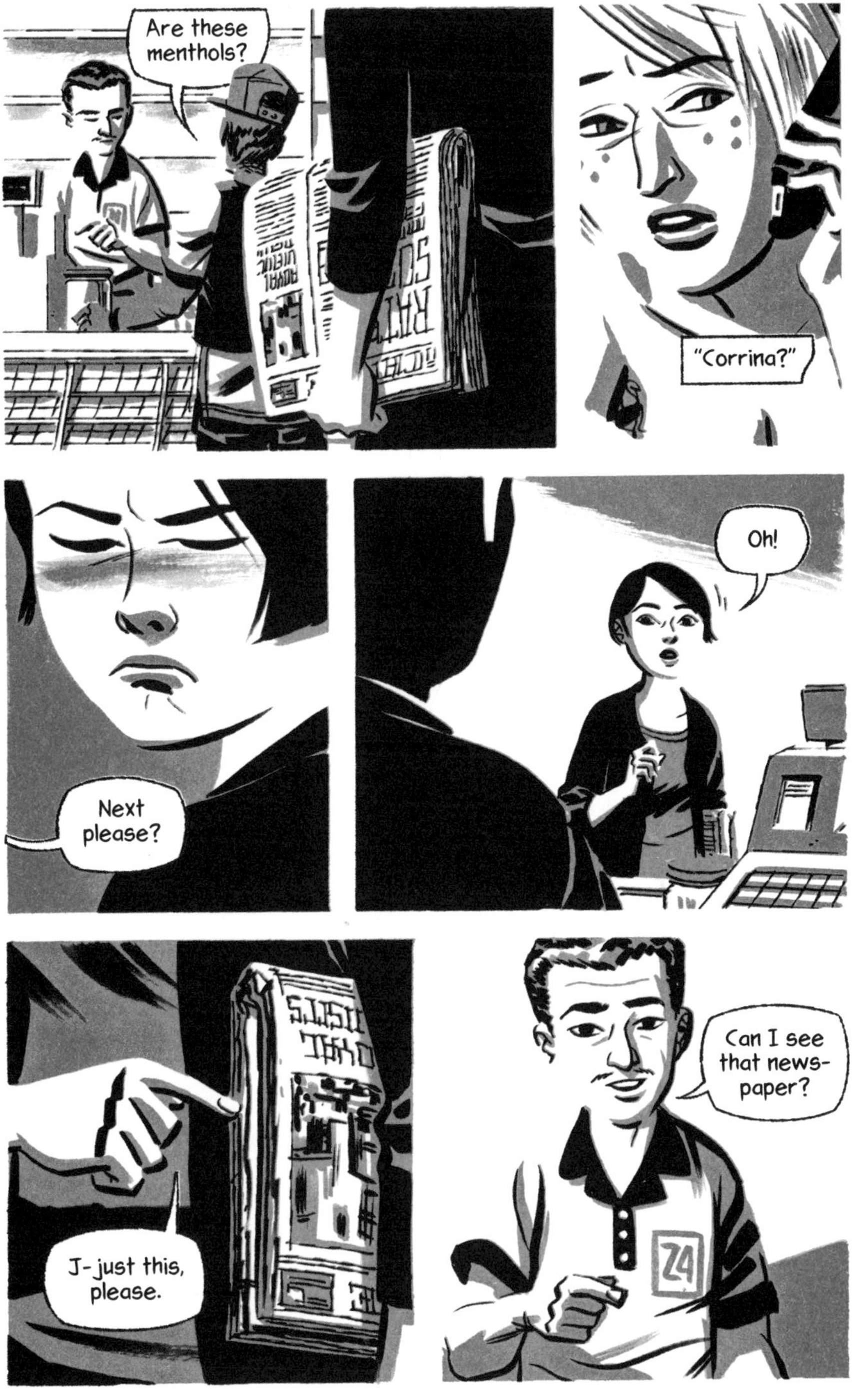
Are these menthols?
"Corrina?"
Next please?
Oh!
J-just this, please.
Can I see that news-paper?
24

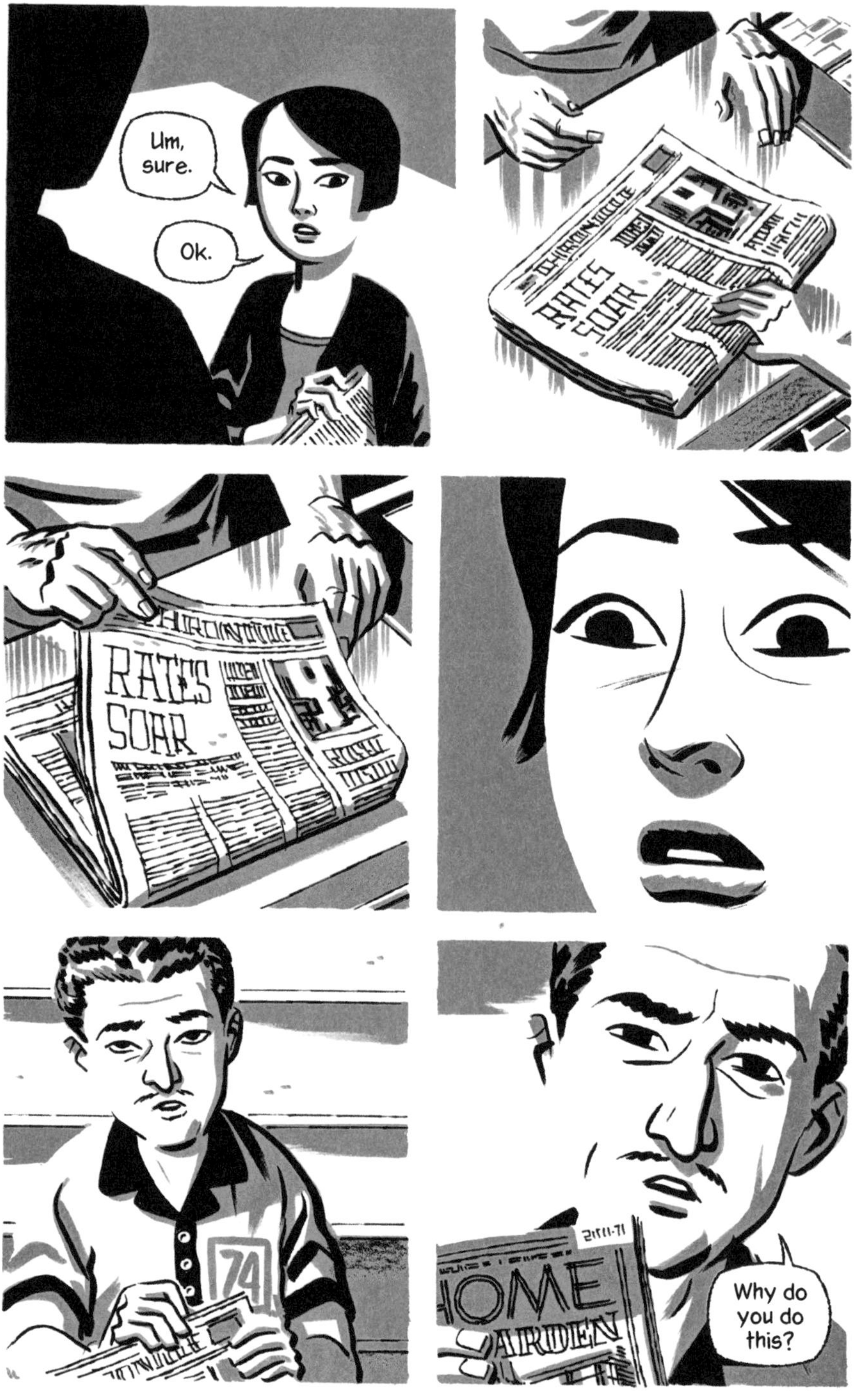
Um, sure.
Ok.
RATES SOAR
RATES SOAR
HOME
Why do you do this?

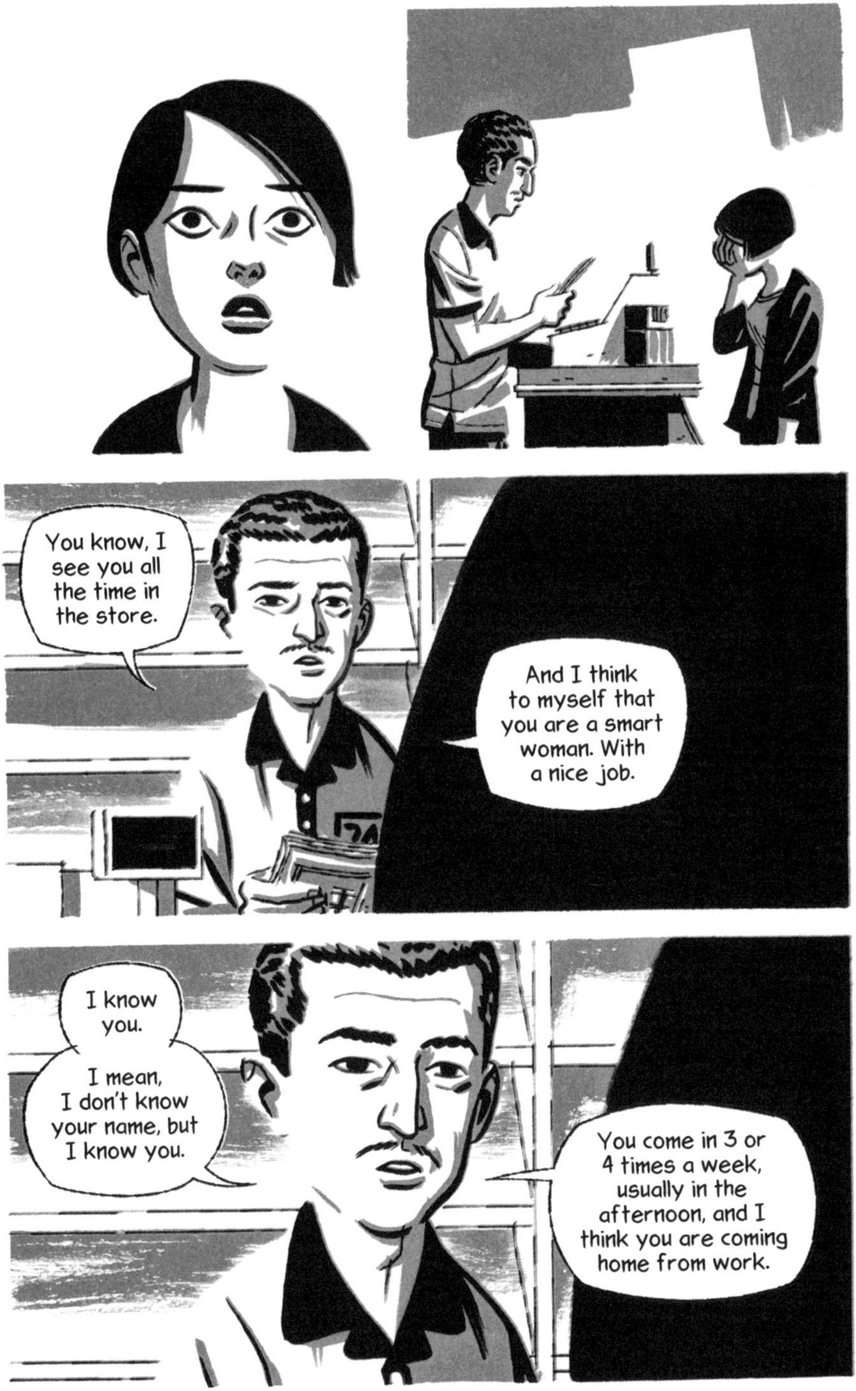
You know, I see you all the time in the store.
And I think to myself that you are a smart woman. With a nice job.
I know you.
I mean, I don't know your name, but I know you.
You come in 3 or 4 times a week, usually in the afternoon, and I think you are coming home from work.

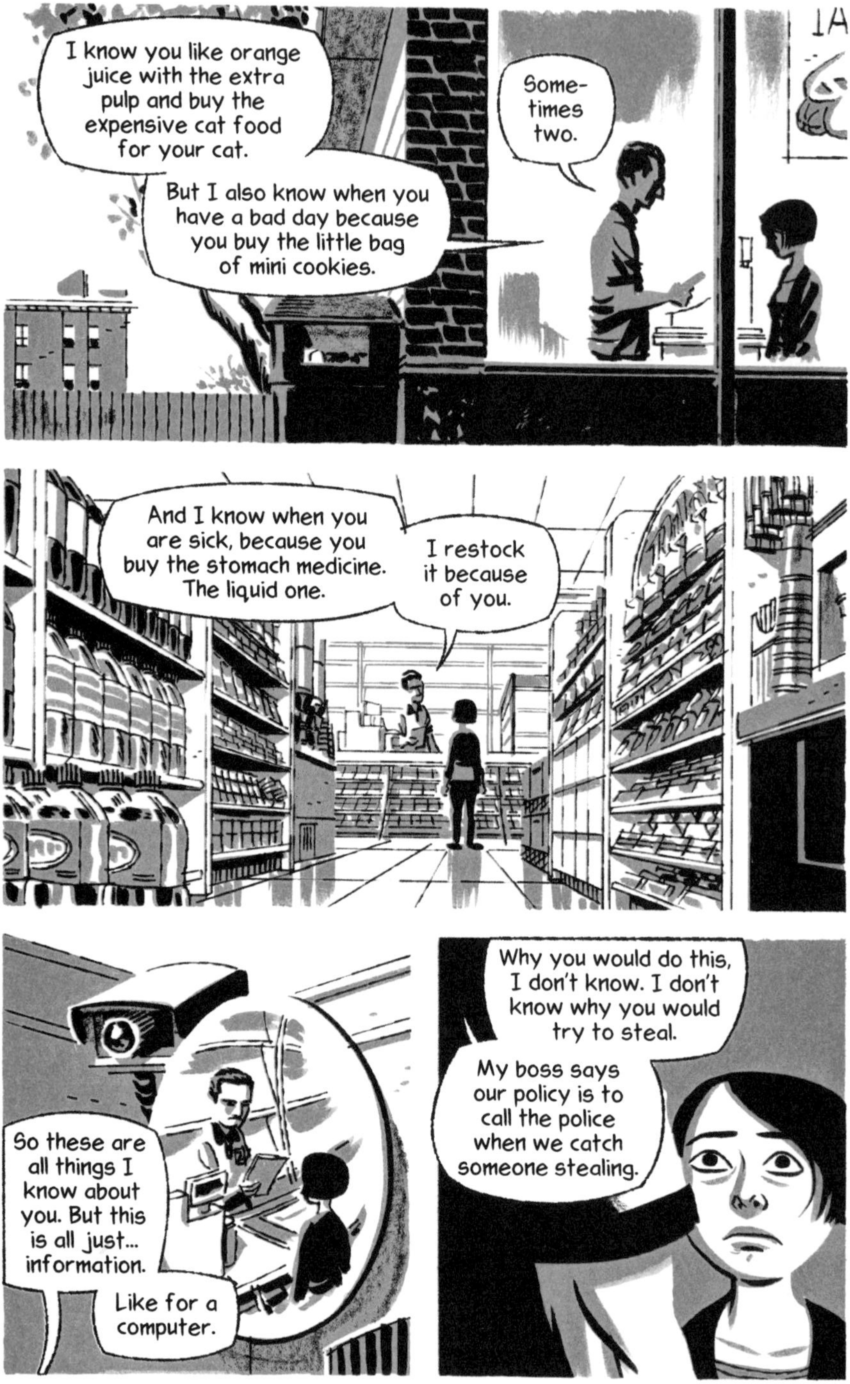
I know you like orange juice with the extra pulp and buy the expensive cat food for your cat.
But I also know when you have a bad day because you buy the little bag of mini cookies.
Some-times two.
And I know when you are sick, because you buy the stomach medicine. The liquid one.
I restock it because of you.
So these are all things I know about you. But this is all just... information.
Like for a computer.
Why you would do this, I don't know. I don't know why you would try to steal.
My boss says our policy is to call the police when we catch someone stealing.

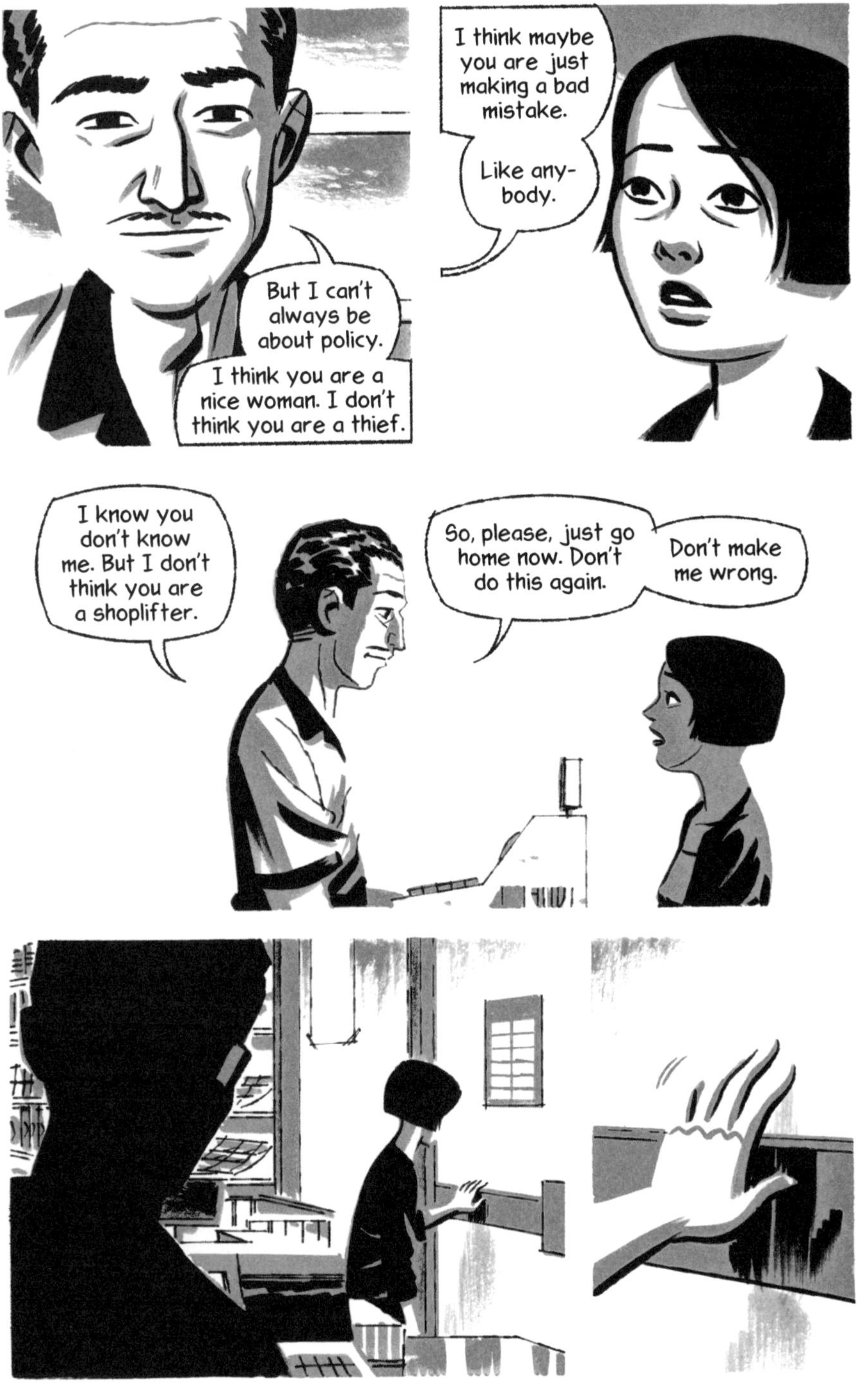
But I can't always be about policy.
I think you are a nice woman. I don't think you are a thief.
I think maybe you are just making a bad mistake.
Like any-body.
I know you don't know me. But I don't think you are a shoplifter.
So, please, just go home now. Don't do this again.
Don't make me wrong.

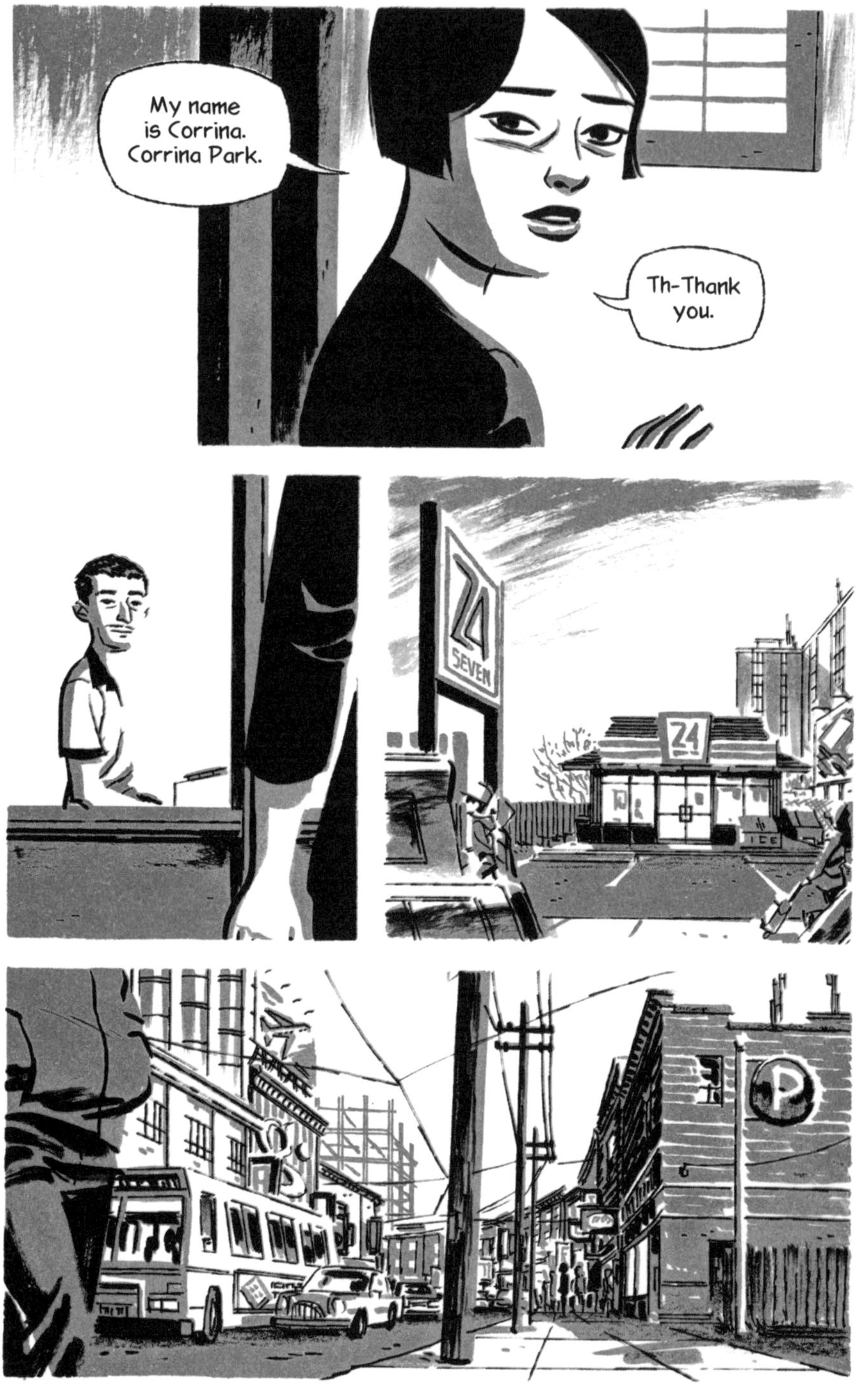
My name is Corrina. Corrina Park.
Th-Thank you.
24 SEVEN
24
ICE

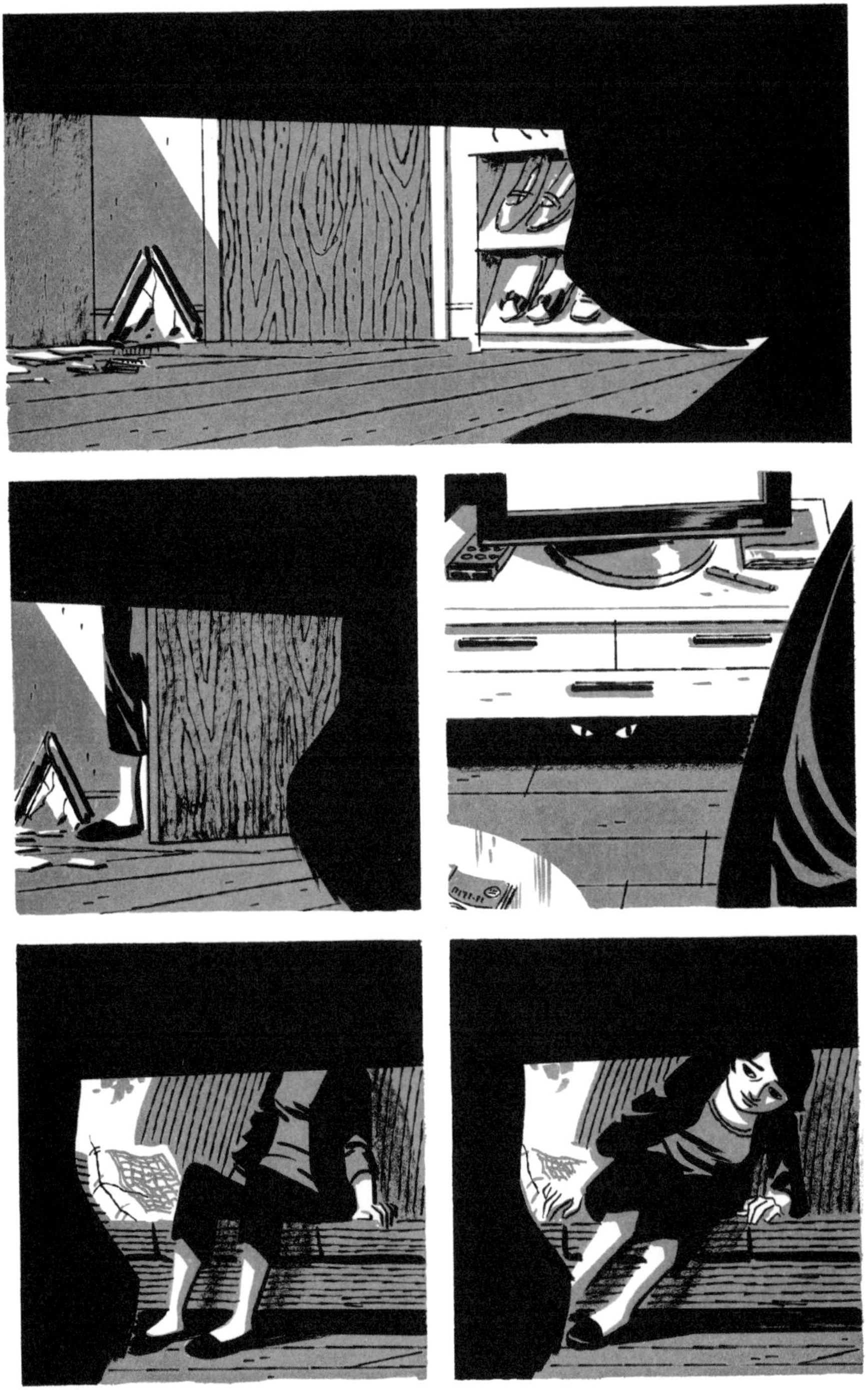

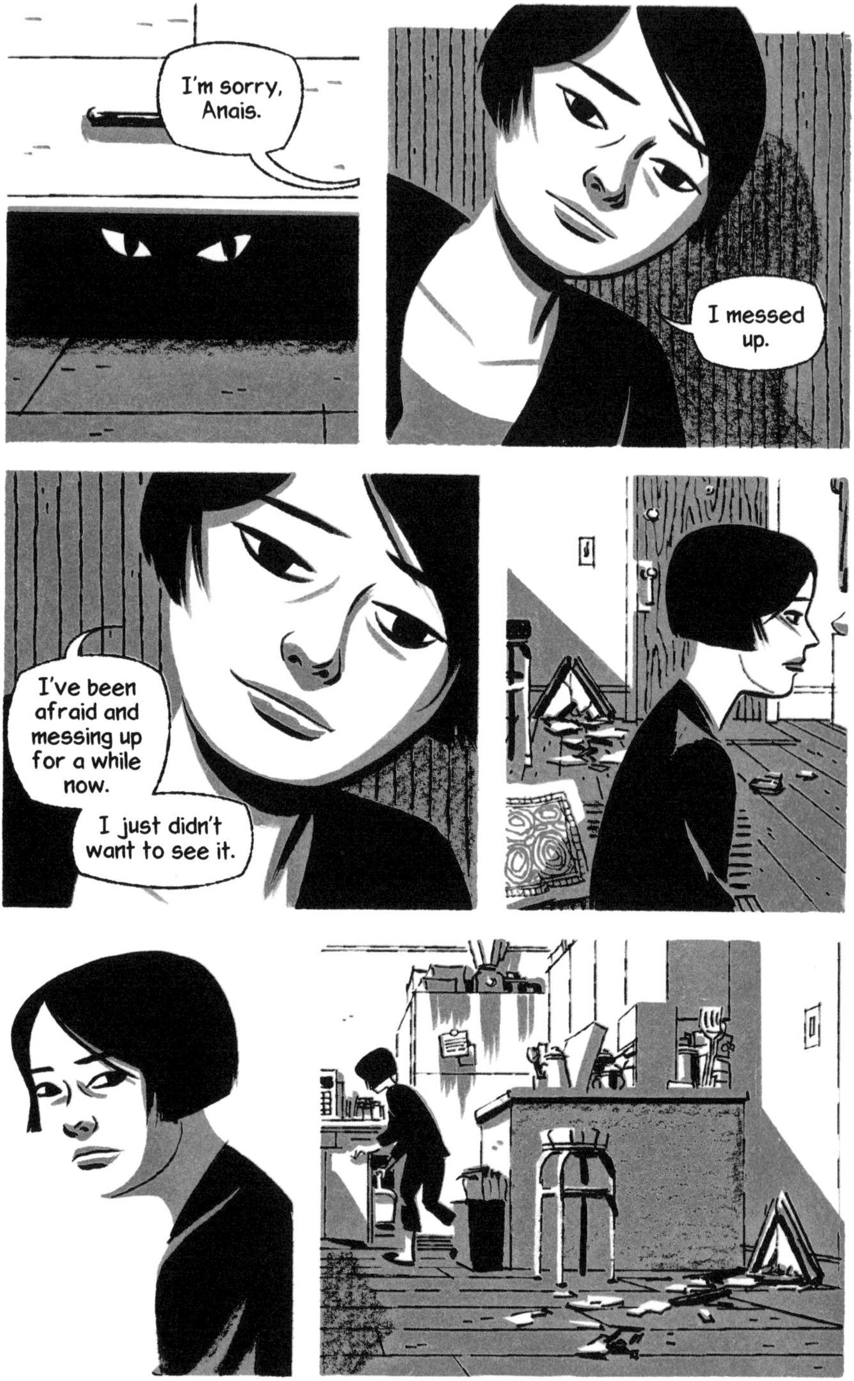
I'm sorry, Anais.
I messed up.
I've been afraid and messing up for a while now.
I just didn't want to see it.

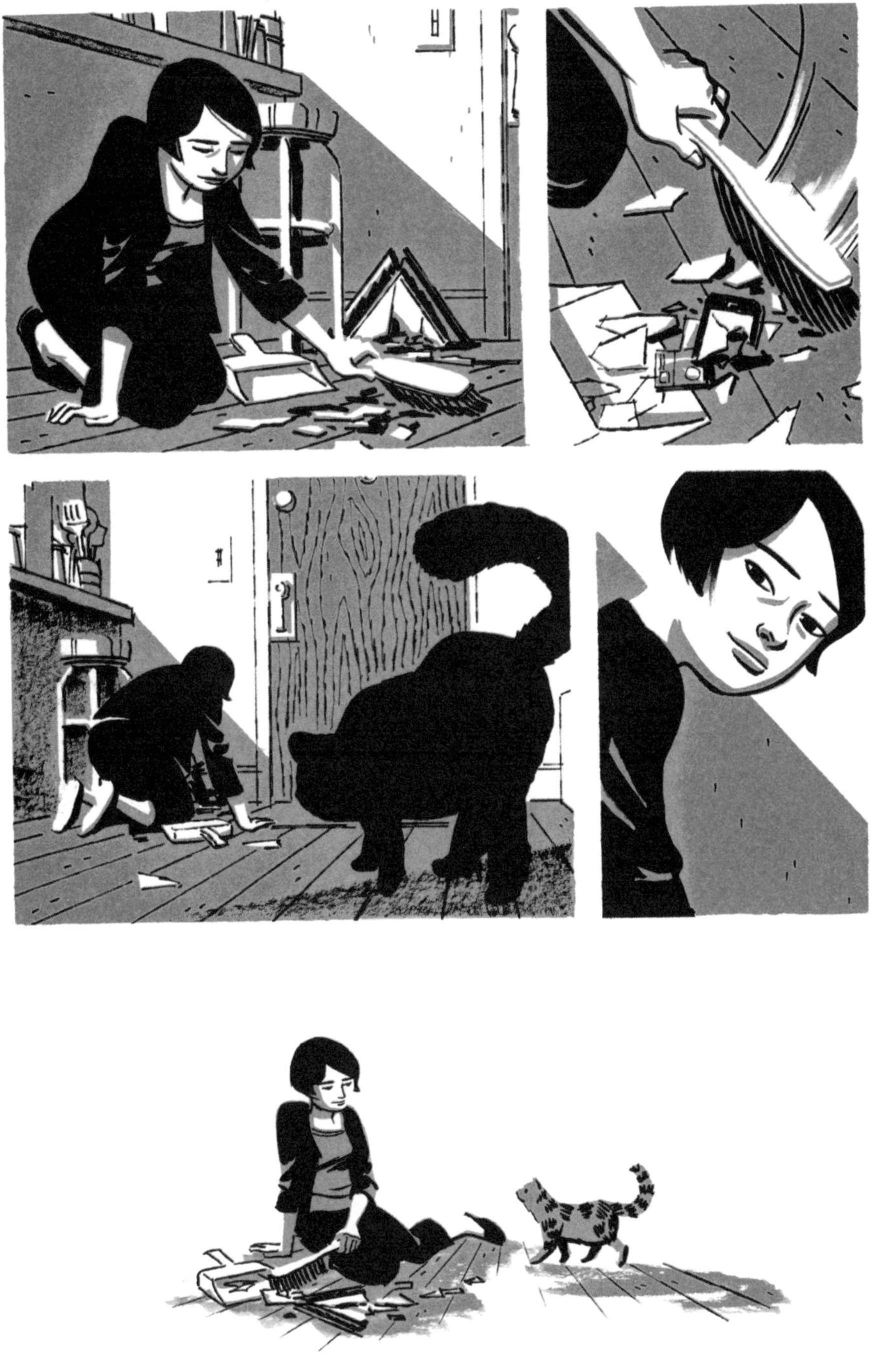

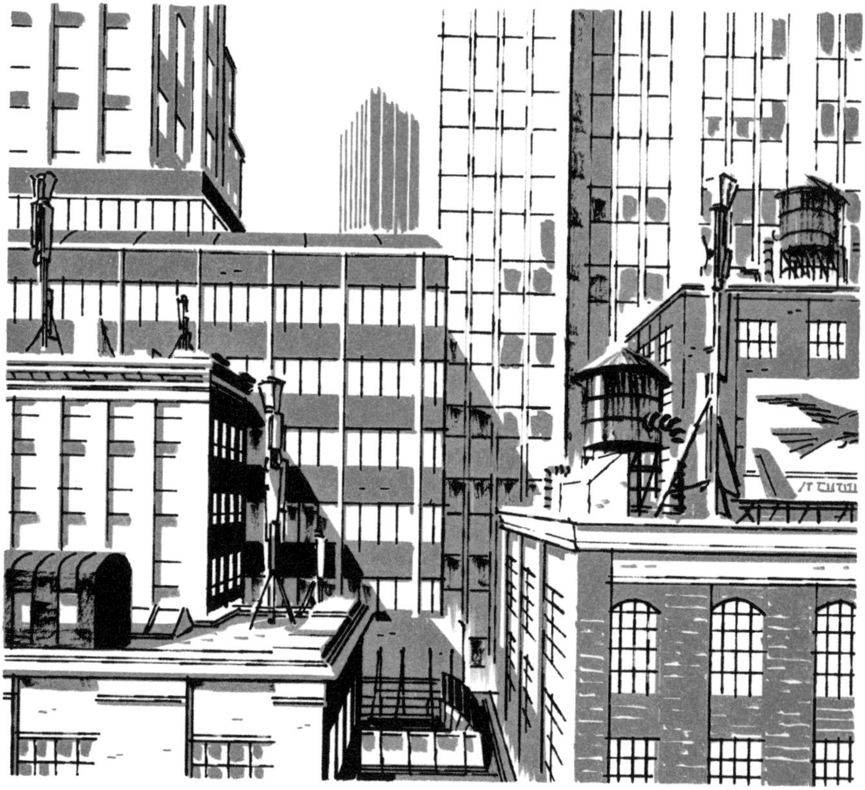

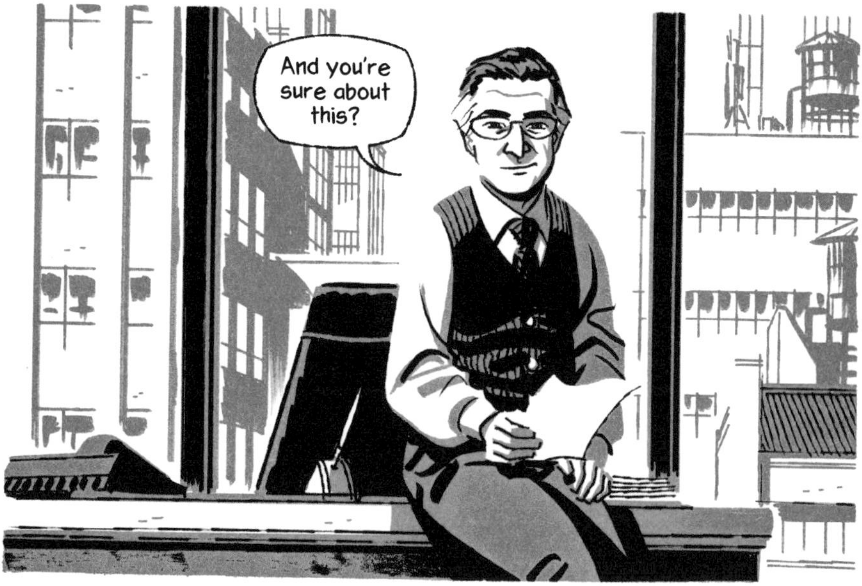
And you're sure about this?

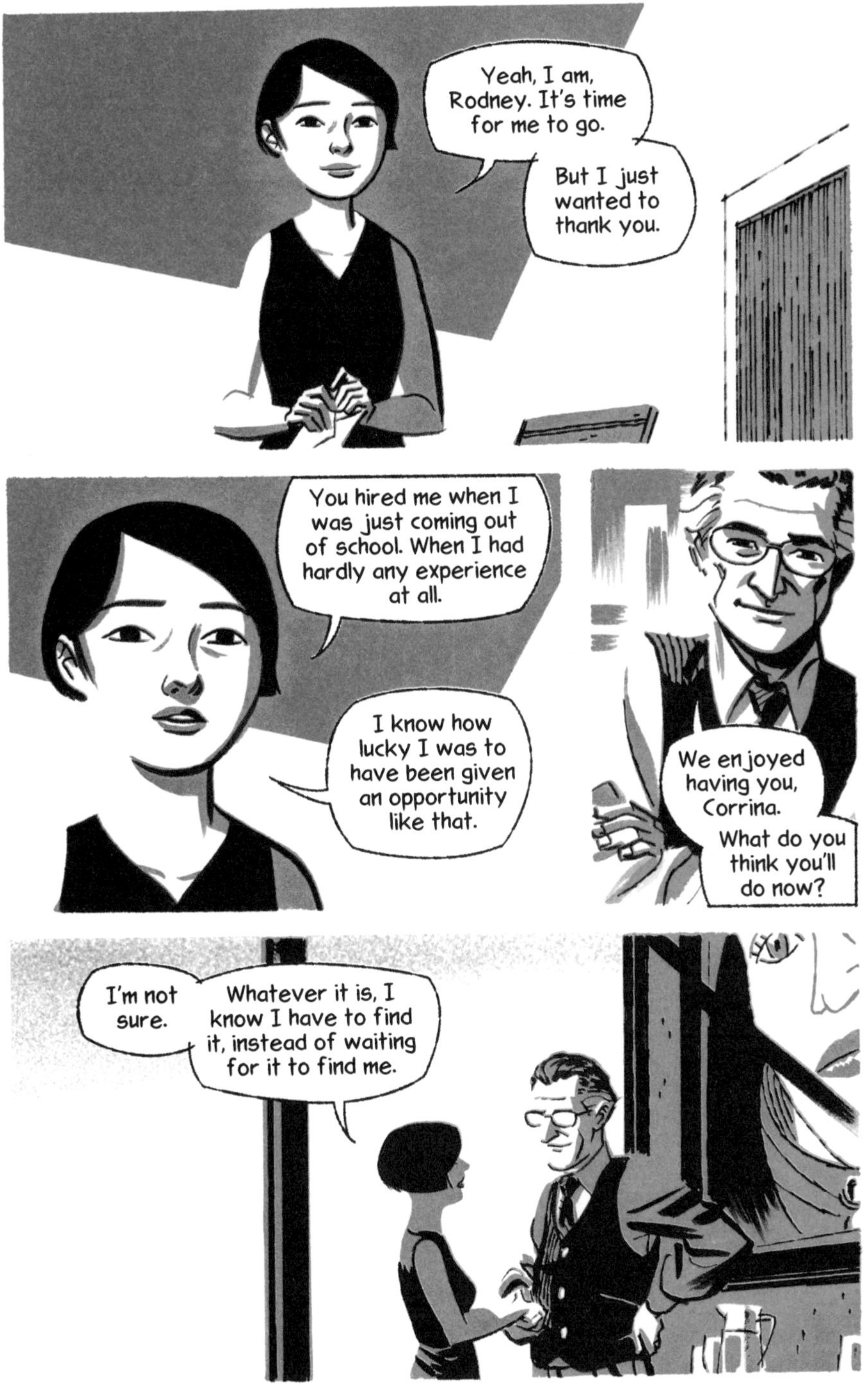
Yeah, I am, Rodney. It's time for me to go.
But I just wanted to thank you.
You hired me when I was just coming out of school. When I had hardly any experience at all.
I know how lucky I was to have been given an opportunity like that.
We enjoyed having you, Corrina.
What do you think you'll do now?
I'm not sure.
Whatever it is, I know I have to find it, instead of waiting for it to find me.

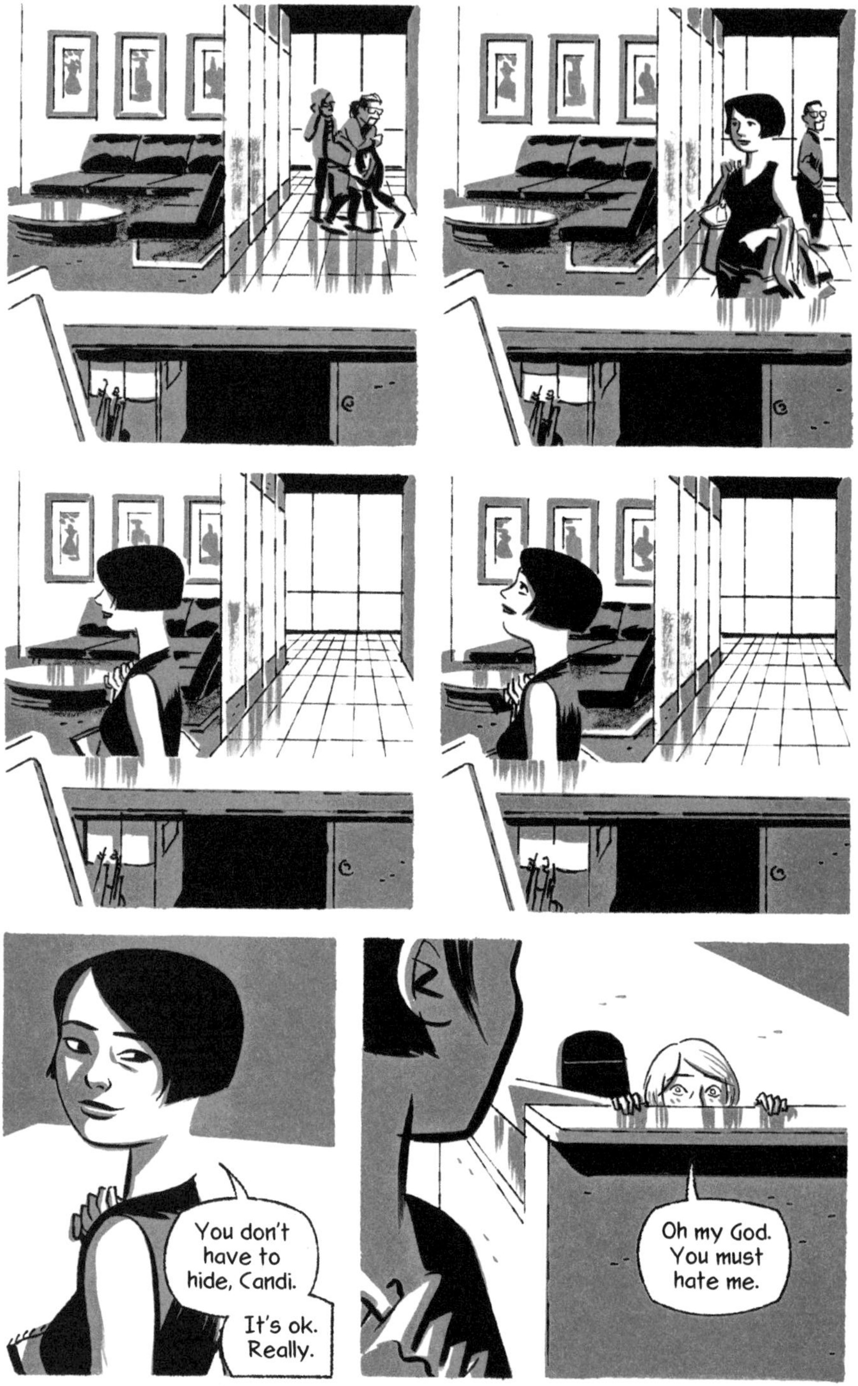
You don't have to hide, Candi.
It's ok. Really.
Oh my God. You must hate me.

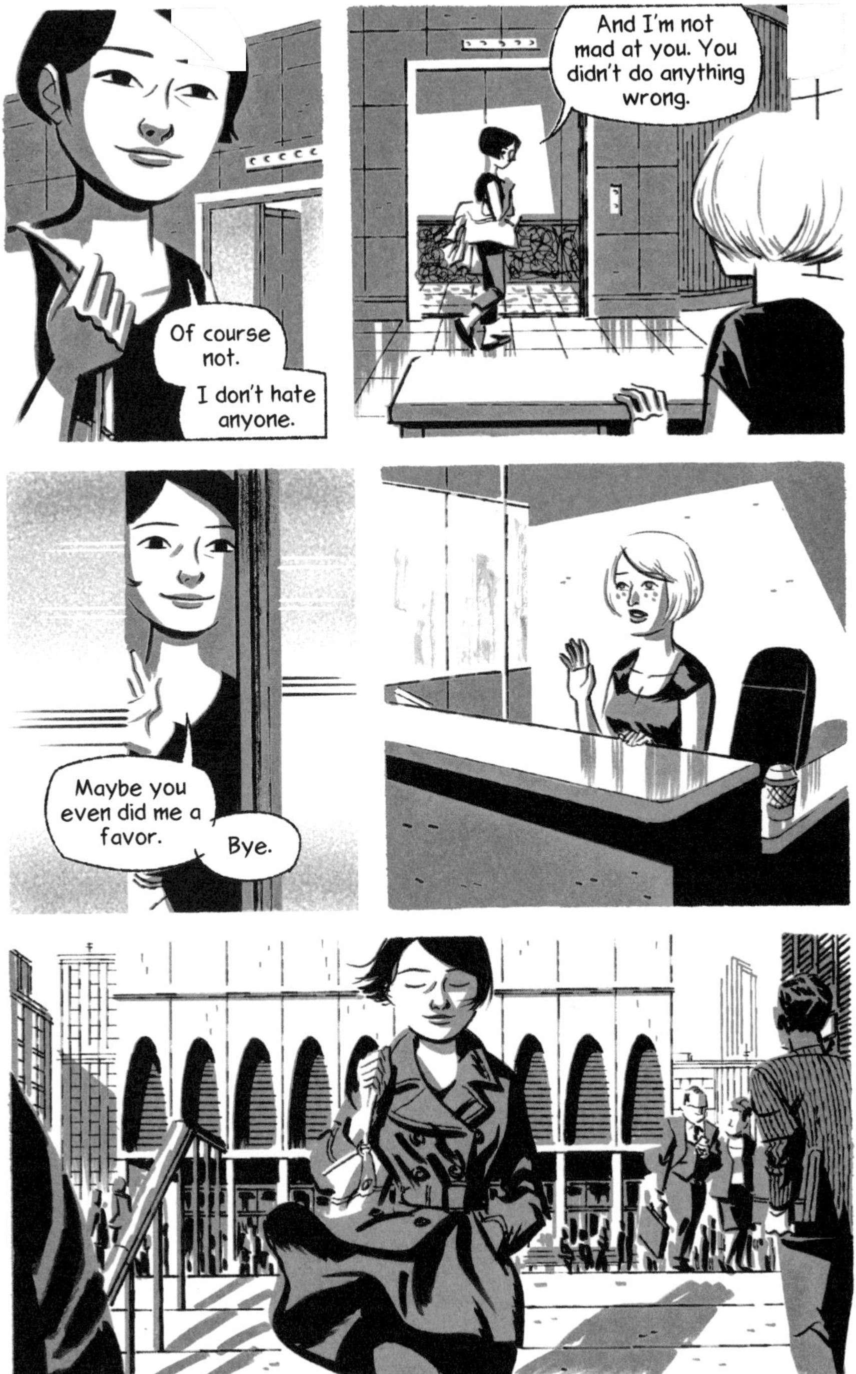
Of course not.
I don't hate anyone.
And I'm not mad at you. You didn't do anything wrong.
Maybe you even did me a favor.
Bye.

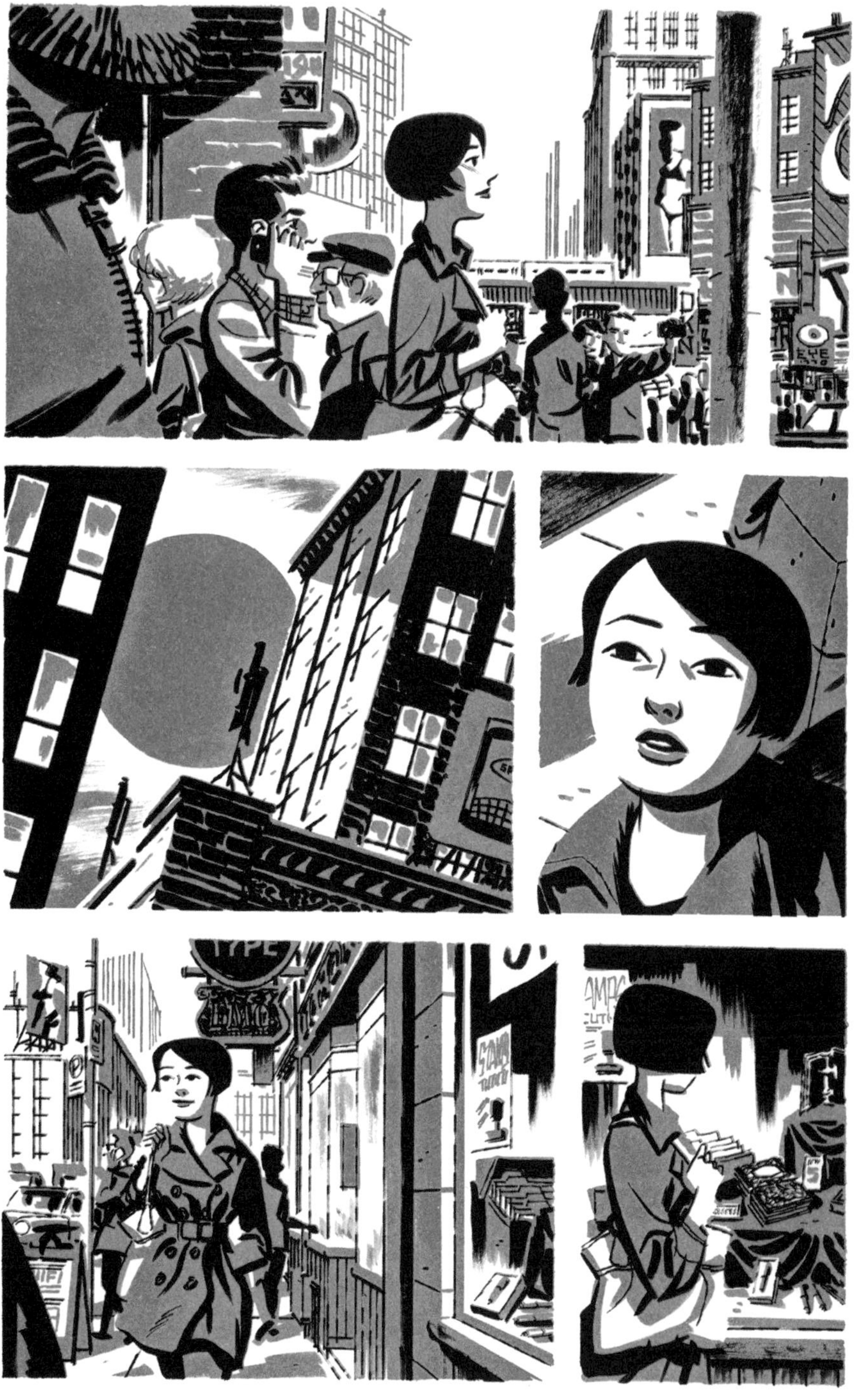
EYE

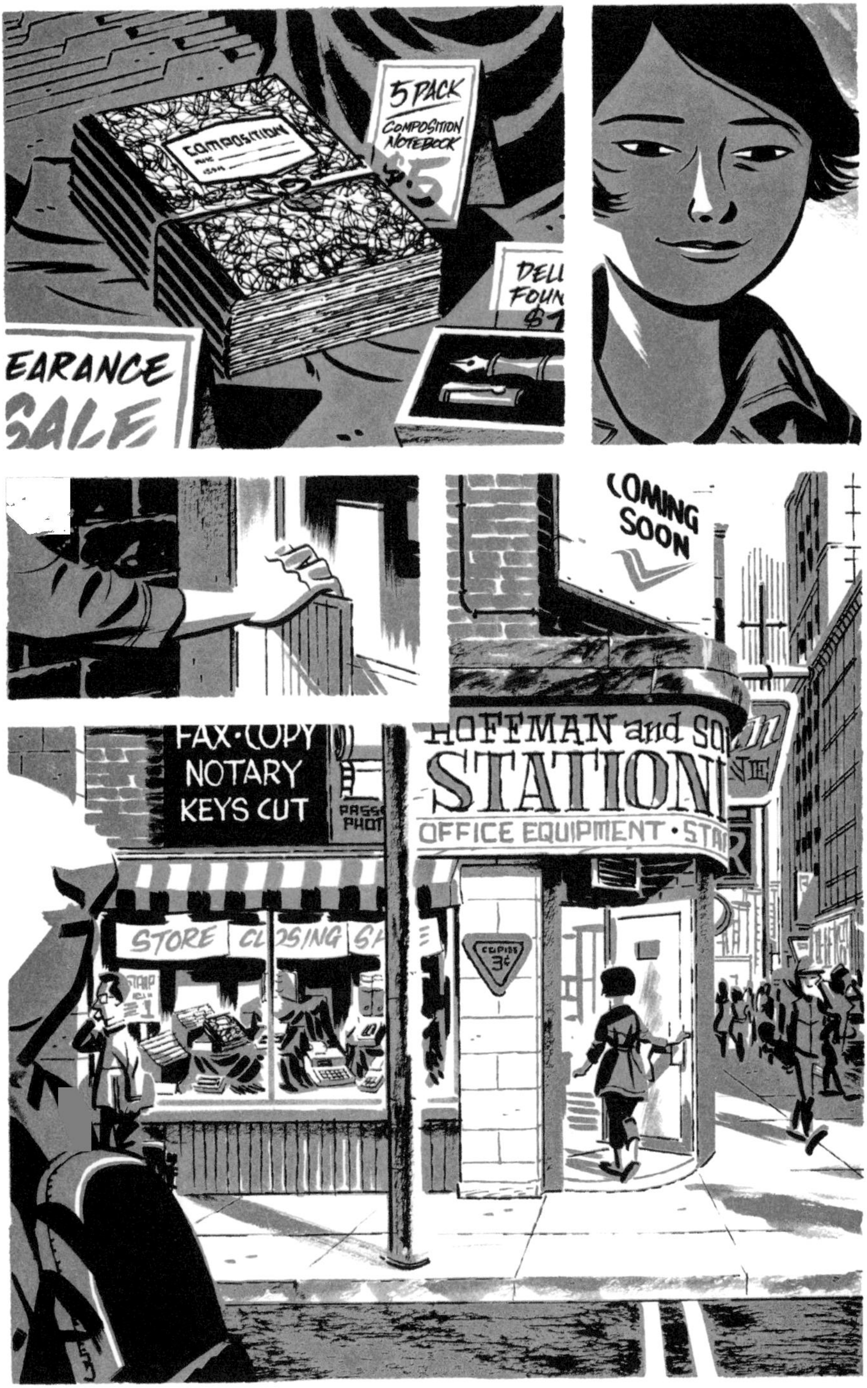

5 PACK
COMPOSITION NOTEBOOK
$5
COMPOSITION
EARANCE
SALE
COMING SOON
FAX·COPY
NOTARY
KEYS CUT
HOFEMAN and SO
STATION
OFFICE EQUIPMENT · STA
STORE CLOSING SA

# Acknowledgments

My thanks go to Chip Kidd for his encouragement and editorial help, Dan Frank and Samantha Haywood for their support and Vincent Bernière for his immense patience. I'd also like to give special thanks to Alex Hoffman and Willow Dawson for their invaluable critiques and to J. Bone and Jay Stephens for lending me their shoulders when I needed it.

As always, the biggest thank you goes to my wife, Claudia Dávila, who worked with me throughout all aspects of this project from writing to art to design. Without her, this book would not have been possible.

**Michael Cho** was born in South Korea but moved to Canada at a very young age. He currently lives in downtown Toronto in a nice house with his wife and daughter, where he spends his days drawing comics and illustrations from his basement studio.